About the Author

Keith Mackenzie Ross is a retired NHS GP; he comes from an artistic family. His mother painted and his father was fond of drawing cartoons for his children. Keith's brother was a fine wood carver and his sister wrote poetry. A niece, Katie, exhibits art in Barcelona; another niece, Jenny, is a well-known potter in Latheron, Caithness, while a third niece, Alice, is a photographer, and her son, Knox Field, is an accomplished sculptor of animal bronzes. Keith himself played keyboard and zither but found practising too difficult so changed to writing. This is his first book.

Tales from a Winchester Hill

Keith Mackenzie Ross

Tales from a Winchester Hill

Olympia Publishers
London

www.olympiapublishers.com

OLYMPIA PAPERBACK EDITION

A CIP catalogue record for this title is
available from the British Library.

ISBN: 978-1-78830-590-7

First Published in 2020

Olympia Publishers
Tallis House
2 Tallis Street
London
EC4Y 0AB

Printed in Great Britain

Dedication

To all those zillions of people who might find this little book fun to read; for even more fun, ask your local croquet club for a free 'taster' session.

Keith Mackenzie Ross, Member of Binchester CC.

Acknowledgements

I should like to thank Dr David Beales, who introduced me to Sara Arnold of Secret Genius, whose genius converted JPEGs to PDFs and, who introduced me to Bevis Hillier, art historian, author and journalist, who ran a rule over the script, advised on copyright and made me trim the cast; to the members of Binchester CC who supported this venture, especially Jan Johnston, Glynis Hassell and Malcolm Faulk and to the distilleries in Islay who allowed me to include excerpts about their activities. These include Bowmore, Bunnahabhain, Ardbeg, Lagavulin, Laphroaig and Bruichladdich distilleries. Also to Sonja Mcguirk, an artiste in her own right, who made me decide if I was writing for a film or a play, or a book, I decided I was a writer of fiction. Also, to Olympia Publishers, who guided me through the process.

Lastly, to my wife, Nita, who despaired of seeing me again when I disappeared into our 'hut'!

PROLOGUE

I was only going to write one tale, but it snowballed until there were ten tales with a full cast of diverse characters. I have linked the tales together to form this little book, though they may be read separately.

The tales are light-hearted, and are about a sport's club, its members, and their activities; they could equally well have applied to any organisation whose members pay an annual subscription. In this case, the sports club is a Croquet Club, (Binchester CC) in the town of Binchester and which is part of a larger Country Club.

As croquet is not well understood, a short description follows:

The game is played on a grass lawn, measuring thirty-five by twenty-eight yards, the size of two single tennis courts. Four hoops are placed five yards in from the corners and two down the middle with a short post placed in the ground between. Four coloured balls (blue, red, black and yellow) are played or hit with a club called a mallet through the hoops in order, the winner being the player to have hit their balls through a designated number of hoops. There are two main forms *Golf Croquet (GC)* and *Association Croquet (AC)* depending on 'how' the balls are hit. Each side (either one or two players) plays with two balls, either blue and black, or red and yellow.

In the text, one or two technical names are used, for example, a *roquet,* where a ball is hit and the player's ball is placed beside the ball which has been hit; the player can then take two extra free shots (*'taking croquet'*). A *bisque* is a term referring to a handicap point. And a *'lift'* occurs when a player's ball is obscured from hitting an opponent's ball (the opponent having been responsible for the position of both balls). The player may then put his ball on a specific point on the boundary, called a *baulk.*

MAIN CHARACTERS

Charles is the author and facilitator of the Tales, and Aunt Agatha is his wife.

The Analyst (Captain of Binchester CC)

Peta and Rocky are staunch supporters of Binchester CC.

Glam, the secretary, and Sam, her husband.

Princess Razzle-Dazzle (the Dazzler, also Agent Y in Chapter four).

Malcolm the Magnificent (also Napoleon and Malcolm Agent X in Chapter four).

General Battlin' Dave (Mercenary and Chairman of Binchester Country Club).

Anne Bee of Islederney.

Annie Gee.

Guest Star Michael (appears as Peter Mikhail Czarevitch - true Pretender and as Sergeant Michel).

Ivan (false Pretender).

OTHER PARTICIPANTS

Appear in order as follows, but may appear in more than one chapter:

CHAPTER ONE

Dimitrian; Johnny and Girl Katerday (his mate); Napoleon and Josephine (Napoleon's wife); Miss Hilary Ballantine (Private Detective); Foreign Agencies: FSB, CIA, BI10.

CHAPTER TWO

Count Anatoli Semenov; President Tyrinov (and his advisers, Yuri Bonetski, Feodor Tcharinko and Yunetski Vamarenko); Tournament Players (Johnny, Peta, Rocky, Ivan, Rich, Perpetuum, The Analyst, Battlin' Dave).

CHAPTER THREE

Members of Binchester CC (Bobbie and Wanda); Committee Members of Binchester Country Club (Messrs Scriabin,

Contract and Shaker); Mr Snodgrass, (Solicitor of Messrs Snodgrass, Inglebasher and Twofingers); Justice Spigot.

CHAPTER FOUR

Nondescript small man; Couriers (Christopher, Agents X, Y and Z; Agent A); President Tyrinov; Stan (Staff of Count Semenov in Hampshire); Colonel Rich (Peter's Controller); Newspaper reporter.

CHAPTER FIVE

Peter Mikhail Czarevitch; Russians (a sergeant, a doctor, an interrogator, a clerk).

CHAPTER SIX

Young Players (Mabayoje, Mustapha, Mohammed, Jeannie, Mathias); Umuru Obasanjo and Abayomi (Mabayoje's parents); Binchester Country Club Committee members; Mr Shortsighted and Ms Knowall make their appearance; Mrs Dotty.

CHAPTER SEVEN

Mac (a retired surgeon); Care Home staff.

CHAPTER EIGHT

Ms Knowall; Bullock Maclean, Frankie (his secretary), Bobbie (Right-hand man to Bullock Maclean), Wanda (Counsellor);

Queen Annie Gee and her girls (Kathleen, Wanda, Moira); her Ladyship Hildegarde Montmorency and Anne Bee (legal beagle, and Chief Clerk at Messrs McMoo & Co); Ben Lyons, a reporter.

CHAPTER NINE

Harriet and Charlie (Glam's friends); Sam and Michael; Ivan, female singer.

CHAPTER TEN

Tatiana and Mishka (victims of a poison attack); Ivan.

NOTE: The heir to a Czar (sometimes spelt Tsar) is called the Czarevitch, and the wife of a Czar is called either Czarina or Czaritsa.
BI10 is British Intelligence; FSB is Russian Intelligence (domestic); CIA is Central Intelligence Agency (USA).

CHAPTER ONE
A Slow Boat to St Helena

INTRODUCTION

Described as a tropical island of unspoiled peace and beauty, St Helena is in the South Atlantic, about level with Brazil. It is around fifty square miles in area and its capital Jamestown overlooks the harbour. Access is by a cruise ship, by a weekly flight from Johannesburg or a monthly chartered flight from Ascension Island. Although an airstrip had been constructed in 2016, it was considered so dangerous because of 'wind shear,' no commercial flight was allowed to land. Since 2017, however, smaller passenger jets have been permitted to land, though the experience may still be nerve shattering. Emperor Napoleon was the island's most famous resident.

AUGUST 2007

A young man, Ivan, and his guardian, Dimitrian – a retired soldier from Russia, arrive on the island. Ivan is eighteen years of age but is called 'the boy'. They are met by a tall, elderly, mustachioed gentleman with greying temples, packing a six-shooter at his waist and multiple medals on his chest. An epaulette announces him to be General Battlin Dave. He takes them to their accommodation, down to the basement in a three-bedroom house built into a hillside, where sufficient food is assembled for a lengthy stay. In one corner is a metal grilled door leading to a storeroom. "Don't go in there," he says, "My ammunition is stored there."

The holidaymakers next arrive in St Helena; a general hubbub ensues.

First, The Dazzler; she is a comely girl with short black hair and short shorts.

She announces in a loud voice, "I put my arm out of the porthole to get some sun, and do you know what? This great big coloured sailor boy came along and dumped his ice cream on it then, he went up to these two girls, you know the ones I mean, the one with the bikini and the other one, and asked them where he was... you'd think he would know his way round his own ship, wouldn't ..."

"Oooh, Dazzler!" said her friend, Glam. Glam is a little different: just below medium height, her hair is at shoulder length, curled at the end, which gives a glamourous look. She wears a holiday type halter dress with flowers and palm trees embroidered on it.

Next was Johnny and Girl Katerday. Johnny is tall and striking looking, like a matinee idol, while Girl Katerday is slim and pretty.

"I do love that snakeskin T-shirt you have on, Johnny," Girl Katerday says.

"Yes, of course, I put it on for..." Johnny admits.

Then came Aunt Agatha and Charles. "I do hate all these vulgar people and their loud voices, Charles. I thought this was a quiet resort."

Hillary Ballantine, private detective arrives in tweeds, looking stern.

There is no sign of the two Annes: Anne Bee and Annie Gee have been friends for many years; dressed in matching Hawaian t-shirts, sizzling hot pants and with their hair up 'bouffant' style, the captain looking through his CCTV screen, says to the officer next to him: "the 'parlour girls.'" The ship's hooter has gone off and they are still in the Passenger's Lounge sipping G & Ts. Annie Gee works in a circus, while Anne Bee owns an Island, Islederney, in the Channel Islands.

Lastly, Peta and Rocky arrive. Peta is slender and neat, while Rocky is very debonair in his trademark tropical kit. "Who on earth is sitting in that corner?" Peta asks: "He looks rather glum!"

"Oh, that is only Napoleon; he is here every day," said the hotel manager, the tall and super talented, The Analyst.

They looked, and in the corner, there, indeed, did sit Napoleon in his greatcoat and two-cornered hat. "Does he say anything?" asked Rocky.

"Oh yes, he comes out occasionally and says 'Hummmmmph!' and then goes back to his corner. And that person, behind the bar, is his maid, Josephine."

The next day, breakfast at the Emperor Hotel was served by Josephine. "Bonjour, tout le monde," she said.

"Sam, I have packed something up for your lunch, so you don't get hungry," Glam announced.

"Gee, thanks," said Sam, a jovial and stocky gentleman, Glam's 'other half', and now dressed for the beach in bathing trunks.

"Good morning, everyone," The Analyst said. "For our

entertainment today, we have skittles, volleyball, clay shooting, orienteering, scuba diving, falconry, bike riding and croquet."

"Croquet!" said Peta. "Why, we play that at home. Binchester in England is where we come from and we should love to play."

"Good," said The Analyst. "We'll all have a shot."

They descended the steep, winding path bordered by oleander, jasmine and tamarisk to the croquet lawn. On the far side was a vertical drop to the ocean, one hundred feet below. Suddenly, somebody screams, and then someone else screams.

"Look! A body on the lawn, and see how awful, skewered by a hoop!"

"Clear everyone away!" called The Analyst. "Don't touch anything."

Miss Ballantine, private detective, was looking closely. "See here, a note with a 'double eagle' on it. It says, 'The Double Eagle has landed.' What can that mean?"

"I think this calls for a drink," said Dazzler. "My, this is exciting. Who'd think that in this little island you could have so much excitement? A Double Eagle? Is it a kind of cocktail?"

"Oooh, Dazzler," Glam exclaims.

"Charles, I think I will faint. When can we go home? My holiday is now entirely spoilt."

"I shall have to report all this, of course," The Analyst said. As the Analyst was also the police chief on the island, he reported it to himself.

Later that morning, the island was swarming with police, and helicopters were buzzing overhead. The croquet lawn was cordoned off, all approaches to the hotel were guarded and any visitor stopped, all staff and guests assembled for questioning.

"Had they seen anything unusual or suspicious, or anyone not known?"

Later, in their room, Aunt Agatha and Charles were sitting drinking their afternoon tea, when Agatha said, "When we went for our walk yesterday, do you remember, Charles? That funny house with the large basement was all shuttered up. Do you think anyone was living there?"

"Why, yes, I remember it well, and that tall bemedaled gunned-up cove outside. I would not like to meet him in a dark alley," said Charles.

"I don't suppose it was anything, but do you think we should mention it?" Aunt Agatha asked.

"No, I don't think so. If we do, we might be here for ages and we do have to get the boat back tomorrow. I booked it after you said you did not like it here."

"I suppose you are right, Charles," said Agatha.

Elsewhere…

"Are you sure he was SVR[1]?" General Battlin' Dave asked Dimitrian.

"Certainly, he was. I spotted him lurking round the hideout and followed him afterwards. Everything he did was classic SVR. It wasn't easy but he had to go."

"But why here? What do they know?" Battlin' Dave asked.

"A good question, my friend. A way back, my ancestors contacted the well-known Russian Semenov family for support. They are still there and they have their backers. It is

[1] The SVR and FSB –Foreign Intelligence Service and Federal Security Service respectively of the Russian Federation, formed from the KGB in 1991, which was formed out of the NKVD in 1954

23

called a 'network'; it is very modern, called Google, but there are eavesdroppers on all this Internet traffic, which is used by the SVR, the CIA and the British BI10. They will know there is something up to do with the restoration of the Czar. My friend, your life is in danger, assuredly, as my name is Dimitrian, you must get away before the investigating forces of the world are on the island. Get the next boat off the island, and then you can escape."

"But what will you do, Dimitrian? Your life will be in danger if you are caught, and the boy too. What will happen to him? Our cause will be as nothing, once he is caught. No one will ever hear of the next Ussuri to be crowned Czar."

"Do not worry, Dave, as you know, we have a plan that will make our cause more likely to succeed. The real Czarevitch is not here, but with our friends in Troitskia. The boy we have here is a false pretender, and will be denounced as an imposter. His DNA will not match the Ussuris. But the world press will be informed and the publicity we get will be enormous, and this will shape world opinion for the return of the rightful Czar. And now, off you go immediately!"

A letter dropped through the letterbox of the *Hideout*. Dimitrian picked it up; someone had just put it through. It read:

I know what you are up to; you won't get away with it. So, give yourselves up. It was signed HB.

"That's very percipient of HB, whoever he or she is. That is exactly what we intend to do!"

By now, the world press had descended on St Helena; Dimitrian, and Ivan, false pretender to the Czar of Russia, made their way to the square outside the Emperor Hotel. "Is there anyone in charge here?" Dimitrian said. In the general melee of press and secret agents, no one seemed to be in control.

"Let us go into the hotel for a coffee then," Ivan said.

They trooped in. The Analyst looked unconcerned. "Good for takings," he said. Napoleon in the corner wondered if there would be a place for him on the next boat out.

"All right, all right then, where are they?" shouted a stern looking man. It was General Battlin' Dave; he had trimmed his moustache and was now wearing a uniform of the UN Officer in Charge, looking very much the part.

"Here we are, sir," Dimitrian replied.

"Well, one of you go with the SVR, that's you, Dimitrian, and you, Ivan, you go with the Brits."

The two Annes did find their way onto the island eventually, but, in the confusion, both missed the boat home, and had to get a later one. They got put under house arrest in Islederney to await Her Majesty's pleasure.

Then, another interruption. "Hey, wait a second, we want a word with them!" In swept the world's press, nearly knocking the UN Officer in Charge, The Analyst and Napoleon off their feet. "We want interviews," they said.

Three hours later, the Emperor Hotel stood empty, and all was quiet, that is, until you listened carefully and heard the clunk, clunk of croquet ball on croquet mallet down on the croquet lawn at the bottom of the winding path.

"That's it. Now, head still, shoulders square, hips back, feet straight, knees bent, right hand down a bit and you can do it," said Dazzler.

"Ooooh, Dazzler!" said Glam.

"I do enjoy this game," Ivan said.

"It is very sociable and skilful," Peta said.

"Come to Binchester Croquet Club when you have said

goodbye to your friends, and we will sign you in. Joining fee is as little as thirty pounds," said Rocky.

"I should certainly love to do that," Ivan replied.

Meanwhile, back at the Emperor Hotel, Napoleon stood up; a pop-up appeared above his head: it said, "It all went wrong!" Then another bigger pop-up appeared, it said, "I was given the wrong information!" Finally, a further much bigger pop-up appeared: it burst. Napoleon had disappeared!

Following the excitement of St Helena when a 'false pretender' to the Russian throne was uncovered, the guests at the Emperor Hotel departed to their various destinations, after taking the return passenger ferry to Cape Town.

Peta and Rocky went home to look after the Binchester Croquet Club.

Glam, Sam and Dazzler returned to the party capital of the universe, Bartley Hintney in Hampshire.

The false or young pretender Czar, Ivan, joined Binchester CC as a new member.

Hilary Ballantine said she was going to follow up a lead to Count Semenov; Napoleon and Josephine were given one week's leave of absence from the island to go to Paris where they had a flat. General Battlin' Dave, the ersatz leader of the UN at St Helena, allowed his name to be put forward to the highest bidder for his services.

The Analyst remained on the island.

Malcolm the Magnificent, member of Binchester CC, had never been away. Immersed in the depths of his cellar, he had been whitewashing its walls, and was now applying the finishing touches. He had been there, maybe six weeks, or maybe six months, maybe even all his life. He couldn't be sure. It was recently he had felt this surreal experience of being in

St Helena as Napoleon, his 'doppelganger' he assumed; he wasn't so sure now he had been in the cellar.

Johnny and Girl Katerday continued on their vacation to Bali before arriving home; they wondered if they should take up roller skating? Johnny had seen roller skaters at breakneck speed on the streets of London. "Could be great fun," he said.

"Could break your neck," Johnny's mate replied.

Aunt Agatha and Charles had gone on to Bahrain for a holiday in the sun. They finally returned home late at night in time to put the cat out and feed their dogs.

Next morning, Charles sighed and woke up. "I had a dream I went on holiday to an island! Do you think that happened? I also dreamt that a young woman was going on a long journey. Can dreams be predictive?"

Aunt Agatha had the last word, "Charles, you do talk nonsense; now, empty the bins!"

CHAPTER TWO
Old Muscovy
September 2007 to April 2016

Miss Ballantine lost no time in starting to trace Count Semenov; she looked up the search engine, Google, and soon found that the Semenovs had originated from Siberia in about 1500. One son, Alexei, had opened a salt mine which became very prosperous and they were granted large areas of land by Ivan the Terrible. They became prosperous merchants developing farming, fishing and mining and did good works supporting the building of Baroque churches and payrolling the Russian Army in the reconquest of Moscow from the Poles. They were raised to the rank of Count by Peter the Great. After the Russian revolution of 1917, the Semenov family estates were seized by the Bolsheviks; the family migrated to the north as part of the 'white army', those who were against the Bolshevik's 'red army', when all trace of them then disappeared.

Such was the dilemma that Miss Ballantine found herself in with no heirs to consult. Miss Ballantine now had a staff of two, the other being her pet Russian wolfhound, and a small legacy. She now set off with her wolfhound to investigate and explore the far north of Russia, hoping there might be some trace of them there. That was where the Semenovs had last been seen.

During the next nine years, in which time, Miss Ballantine, plus dog, endured terrible privation and hardships in their unenviable quest to find a trace of the modern Semenovs. They eventually came across a peasant in a remote township in the far, far north of the country, who casually mentioned the word '*Semenovskogo dvorca*' and '*Kunetsov S*'; he was the local historian and suggested that if they went to St Petersburg and looked up the library there, they might find what they were looking for.

By this time, Miss Ballantine had no money, but with a smattering of Russian she was able to hitch herself a sleigh ride to near St Petersburg. Reaching the library, she was astonished to find a section entitled 'Descendents of Semenov'; even more so, to find an address near Moscow with the name of Troitskia.

While Miss Ballantine was embarked on her perilous mission to trace the roots of Count Semenov between 2007 and 2016 at Binchester CC, croquet continued in an uninterrupted sequence of springs, summers, autumns and winters; weekly *mixins* took place, and summer competitions were held, with many folks complaining that the prizes were always won by the same people. Ivan stayed with Peta and Rocky for a year, and then went to live in London. He joined the City Dance Club to learn 'ballet'. He returned to Binchester at weekends to play croquet. Membership continued at about forty-five members. For Charles and Aunt Agatha, life became a routine.

TROITSKIA MONASTERY NEAR MOSCOW, MAY 2016

The Troitskia Monastery was one of the most revered sites in Russia; armies were blessed here before going to war. As a result, many Czars, if they were victorious, had left their wealth to the monastery. The monastery itself was surrounded by a forty-foot-high wall over one mile in length surrounding the entire site.

Count Semenov had his estates restored to him on the downfall of the Soviet Union but had to keep a low profile on account of his family's past record and the 'secret' he was holding.

Here and outside in the countryside, Count Semenov exercised his prize pedigree Russian wolfhound dogs, known for their loyalty and hunting qualities. Here, also resided the alleged true pretender to the Russian throne, Peter Mikhail Czarevitch, great grandson of Czar Ussuri. Peter was unusually tall for his age. At sixteen, he was six feet seven inches. As he filled out, he had the bearing of a Czar. Athletic, powerful and energetic, he helped with the dogs, but also took a keen interest in shipbuilding, like his illustrious namesake, Peter the Great, in the 17th century, who was also of great stature.

It was in these surroundings that one day a note was passed through the door of Count Semenov's residence, addressed to Count Anatoli Semenov. Peter received this note it read:

I know what you are up to; you won't get away with it. It was signed simply 'HB'.

"I have heard of this person from the TV," Anatoli Semenov said. "It is the famous English detective, Miss Ballantine. I wonder what she wants? Ask her in."

Miss Ballantine was ushered in.

"Welcome, Miss Ballantine," Anatoli Semenov said. "We tend to agree with you. The Russian people may want their Czar back but President Tyrinov will not have it. Tomorrow, we are going to Truffles, the famous English dog show, where we have entered our Russian wolfhound. Perhaps, you would like to come with us. My private Trilander plane is ready and waiting at Moscow Airport. It will save you a lot of trouble if you do."

"I should love that," Miss Ballantine replied.

THE KREMLIN, MAY 2016

Seated by the large boardroom table in the Party Polit Bureau office, Vladimir Tyrinov was surrounded by his Security Committee, Chief of Staff, Yuri Bonetski, Head of Security, Feodor Tcharinko, and Foreign Minister, Yunetski Vamarenko.

Vladimir was built like a middle-weight boxer, but without the 'cauliflower' ears and his jacket also seemed a little too tight. He opened the discussion, "My astrologers tell me that not far from Moscow there is a man who calls himself the true pretender to the Czar. What do you make of it, Yuri?"

Yuri and the others looked like heavy-weight boxers, but their suits did fit. Yuri crossed and uncrossed his legs, "We have had him under surveillance for several years. Initially, there was little to emerge, until the last year, when the name, Peter Mikhail Czarevitch, began to be mentioned. As soon as we heard that he was six feet seven inches tall, we became more interested on account of his predecessor, Peter, sometimes called 'The Great', by our more reactionary comrades. At this stage, we kept him under 'highest alert'. This did not incriminate him, so we sent in our public health team and took samples of blood for DNA on the pretext of a public health program. The results are conclusive: he is indeed who he says he is; he is related to the ancestors of the putative Czar Ussuri."

The silence was palpable in the room. The chairman said, "What do you think, Feodor?"

"I think we should bring him in," Feodor replied.

"And you, Yunetski?"

"I agree," he said.

"Very well then, Yuri, I think you should drop in and bring him in for questioning. That is all, comrades."

Early next morning, a party of specially trained paratroopers, parachuted into Count Semenov's residence in the Troitskia Monastery. Alas, there was no one there, the house was empty.

Yuri reported back to the Party Chairman.

"You fool!" Vladimir said. "Find him, or else we shall be interrogating you!"

"Yes, comrade, sir!" the once confident, but now shaken, Yuri replied.

TRUFFLES DOG SHOW, NATIONAL EXHIBITION CENTRE, BIRMINGHAM, ENGLAND, JUNE 2016

The biggest dog show in the world, entrants have to pass strict controls of class and health before being accepted. Overseas entrants have to win overseas competitions. There are two hundred classes of dogs and only the four best in each class gain an entry. Count Semenov had entered his Russian wolfhound, once favoured by Czars for their hunting ability and now renowned for their elegant sleekness as a fashion icon in the home.

All the entry and exit gates were heavily guarded and policed by security officials, some in uniform, some in different uniforms denoting different organisations; others were in plain clothes. Who did they represent? Were they SVR, CIA or BI10 or even private organisations? Ordinary spectators were searched for hidden items; perhaps liquids, anything that might be considered a hazard. It was quite intimidating. By the time one arrived at one's seat, the thought was, 'Was it worth it?'

At one gate, a smartly dressed lady in a French beret, striped T-shirt and matching trousers arrived. She allowed herself to be searched and took her place in the front row opposite the judges. She was Miss Ballantine, special entry permit arranged by Count Semenov.

Two pairs of eyes were high up in the roof on the walkway, looking down with binoculars: Count Semenov and Peter Mikhail Czarevitch

The judging had begun; each dog in its category was paraded through the ring, the judges at the side with their clipboards noting every waggle, every wiggle, the bearing of each dog. Then they would come over and examine the dog, its teeth, head and general symmetry and walk back making their marks on the clipboard.

After a while, the examiners conferred and the senior judge then took the microphone and announced to the public and to loud applause the winner of the class.

Each class of dog was examined in the same way; the judging took three hours, until finally the turn came of the

Truffles 'Best of Show'. The Count had won his class and was in the final group for the Best of Show Award.

There were twenty dogs; the Count's dog was last; he was walked round the show ring by one of the Count's assistants. At last, the result was announced. The winner… was the Russian wolfhound! Much applause. The Count looked satisfied. They had a way of doing this in Russia!

Then, suddenly, two loud noises like fireworks were heard; the entire audience either screamed or looked startled and everyone all moved out into the middle of the arena, marshals, CID, security officials, audience, judges – mayhem ensued! It was later established that two cars in the car park had backfired – or was there another reason, perhaps?

Count Semenov and Peter hurried down from their perch and into the arena to retrieve their dog and the trophy. Peter's great height made him noticeable; he struck two men down who tried to approach him. Gathering up their animal and cup, they found their way out to the waiting limousine which was to take them to their residence.

"That all went, well – according to plan, I would have thought," the Count observed. They were driven back to their location: 5 Hyde Park Gate, London.

Later next day, Anatoli and Peter Mikhail, having been driven home the previous night from the NEC Birmingham, were having breakfast. Their pet Russian wolfhound was sleeping peacefully by their feet, oblivious of the previous day's adventures.

Anatoli Semenov said to Peter Mikhail, "Peter, it is too dangerous for you to return to Troitskia; they know who you are and where you live."

"I agree," Peter the true Czarevitch replied. "I must give

myself up and rely on a people's revolution."

"No, that will not work; they will never allow that. You will be eliminated, and that will be the end. No, you must become incognito. You are good at that. I suggest...um... yes," he hesitated awhile, "You could, er, perhaps join the Foreign Legion for a time!"

"I hadn't thought of that, but a good idea, Anatoli; I will be safe there. I will make arrangements tomorrow for a one-year contract," Peter Mikhail, the Czar true Pretender sounded confident of this plan.

"Very well then, that is agreed. And now I have to make arrangements for myself. I have been getting texts and emails from people wanting to buy Russian wolfhounds. I have asked my agent to find me a place in the UK where I can breed them and they have come up with a nice estate in Hampshire near Binchester. It has outdoor and indoor swimming pools, outdoor and indoor tennis courts, and outdoor and indoor croquet lawns. It has one thousand acres, ten bedrooms and ten bathrooms. I can commute from one place to the other. Maybe, however, it is too small, Peter?"

"No, I think just that's about right, Anatoli," Peter the Czarevitch said.

"Now what shall we do tonight? We have some time on our hands. I have been looking at the 'What's on' and there is a professional croquet tournament at the O2 Arena. That could be interesting."

"What a good idea, Anatoli. I will get some tickets. They are not inexpensive at fifty pounds to one hundred pounds each. But, first of all, we must have supper beforehand at some nice restaurant!"

Later, after a pleasant supper, Anatoli and Peter were

seated in a box overlooking the O2 arena; they perused the programme.

THE O2 ARENA PROFESSIONAL CROQUET TOURNAMENT PURSE £500,000 POUNDS

The top players were there: Rich, Perpetuum, The Analyst (over from St Helena), Peta and Rocky, Johnny and Ivan, now living in London and for whom it was just a short journey to the O2 arena, with guest star, General Battlin' Dave. The Count laughed when he read that Perpetuum was called Perpetuum because he was always on the move! They were to play one round of thirteen-point *Golf croquet* (GC for short) one round of fourteen-point *Association Croquet* (AC for short), followed by an interval and then the semi-finals for the two events (GC and AC, respectively). The final of the two winners of the semi-finals to play three rounds of *One-Ball*, (ie one ball for each player). All matches to be timed – only fifteen seconds allowed between the end of one turn and the beginning of the next turn.

The first round began: on the first corner were Rich and Perpetuum. Perpetuum, the Count noted, was small in stature and wore a baseball cap, as opposed to Rich who was quite large all round and wore a Panama hat. Perpetuum bounded on to the court, did a 'stretching' routine, a couple of cartwheels, some 'push-ups' and was ready. Rich put his first shot in front of hoop one; Perpetuum knocked it out from twenty yards. Rich put his second shot in front the hoop again and Perpetuum hit his ball through the hoop off Rich's ball. Score one-nil to Perpetuum. Rich won hoop two and the next four hoops were halved, and the score was level at five-five and then six-six.

The final hoop, hoop thirteen, the *Golden Hoop*; Perpetuum promoted his second ball to one foot on the far side of the hoop; too good for Rich, and Perpetuum won seven-six.

"Great game," Anatoli Semenov said.

Next up were The Analyst and Rocky; the game went to form; The Analyst won seven-four.

Anatoli Semenov explained how the *Association* games were played to Peter Czarevitch; by hitting another ball, you got two extra shots and you could do this once off all the other balls in order to get your ball through the next hoop. This saw convincing wins for Peta, who beat Johnny fourteen-nil, and Battlin' Dave, who beat Ivan by the same score.

The interval was next; Glam, Sam and Dazzler had decided to come and watch this, the first professional tournament they had seen. While sipping their Daquiries, Glam noticed an emblem they had seen on another occasion in another place. A very tall young man standing next to them was wearing a jacket with, in the lapel, a badge with a 'double eagle' on it. "I am sure I know him," Glam said.

Dazzler looked around. "Well, I don't know; is he a Russian croquet player too? And who is the other gentleman who is with him? They all seem to know each other. Is Ivan a friend of his, I wonder?"

"You remember the 'double eagle' on the fellow who was killed at St Helena? There is something very fishy going on here!"

"I thought Peta shouldn't have played her first shot like that, didn't you think?"

Glam said, "Ooooh, Dazzler. It is time to return to our seats!"

The second half of the first Professional Croquet Tournament brought The Analyst against Perpetuum in the first semi-final (GC section). Perpetuum got off to a great start by winning the first five hoops before The Analyst got a grip on the situation. He had not played during the Christmas break, but now, suddenly finding his form, created a sensation by winning the next seven hoops and running out the winner.

In the second semi-final (AC section) Peta was to play Battlin' Dave; Battlin' Dave suddenly, however, had lost all his form of the morning and easily lost to Peta – fourteen-nil.

The final saw Peta v Analyst, a great line-up, everyone thought. Peta won the first game with a perfect two-ball break through all thirteen hoops; The Analyst responded with an equally brilliant two-ball break to win the second game. Now for the third game – who was to prevail? The Analyst won the toss, straight through the first hoop, up to the second, through that with his free stroke and a perfect approach to hoop three. Peta 'blobbed' hoop one. The Analyst is again through hoop three, up to hoop four and through that. He laid up on the boundary. Peta could only get into position for hoop one and The Analyst again played safely. Peta went through hoop one, up to hoop two and through to hoop three. The Analyst played up to hoop five and Peta is through hoop three and *roquets* The Analyst. Peta's *croquet* shot, and *continuation* shot takes her through hoop four and now she has a two-ball break. Will she finish? Peta is through hoops five, six, seven, and eight but placed awkwardly for hoop nine, so she plays a defensive shot sending The Analyst up to corner two and she plays up to hoop nine, but wait, has she left a '*lift*'? She has, and The Analyst playing from a *Baulk* point *roquets* Peta, then plays a brilliant *croquet* shot and like Peta, has a two-ball break; he goes through hoops five, six, seven, eight, nine, ten and eleven but then loses control! Peta is on the north boundary but hits in brilliantly and also has a two-ball break, scores nine, ten, eleven and in her anxiety, 'blobs' hoop eleven. The Analyst hits in and wins.

"What an exciting game!"

After the event, Anatoli and Peter went to have a drink; also having a drink were Ivan, the young pretender, Peta and Rocky. Peter, the true pretender, noticed the young pretender's lapel with the double eagle badge on it. "Hello," he said. "You must be the false pretender."

"And you must be the true pretender. What do you do now?" Ivan asked.

The true pretender said, "I am joining the Foreign Legion on a one-year sabbatical to Africa. I cannot claim to be the Czar right now, because there is another man who thinks he is the Czar, Vladimir Tyrinov."

All three dogs are destined to each have their day!

CHAPTER THREE
No Free Lunch
July 10th, 2016

It is Saturday morning at Binchester CC; Bobbie and Wanda are playing '*golf*' croquet together with Anne Bee, and Annie Gee, all members of Binchester CC. "Did you have a good trip home, Anne Bee?" asked Wanda.

"I had a lovely time in St Helena, until I got involved in a fracas with some Russians outside the hotel and who got arrested after a drinking session. Annie Gee got arrested too and put under 'house arrest' by some bolshie General. I had to claim 'diplomatic immunity!' Otherwise, we might be still under surveillance!"

"Well, how exciting!" Wanda said.

"It's your turn."

A little later, a very smart foreign looking gentleman appeared with a large dog. "It's quite safe; he won't hurt you. Let me introduce myself. I am Anatoli Semenov and I live near here and having two croquet lawns at my house, I am wishing to play more competitively. I thought I should come to your lovely lawns. May I join you? Incidentally, this is my pet

Russian wolfhound. Sit down, Strog!"

So, Anatoli Semenov and Anne Bee, Annie Gee, Bobbie and Wanda played some *golf* croquet.

"You are a bit too good for us, Anatoli, I will introduce you to the secretary and he will give you an application form to join our club. It is only thirty pounds for the first year," Bobbie said.

"Oh, I think I can manage that; I thought you might say one thousand pounds!" Anatoli replied.

"Well I never," Annie Gee exclaimed.

THE BOARDROOM AT BINCHESTER COUNTRY CLUB. JULY 16th, 2016

In his blog, General Battlin' Dave describes the many roles he plays: He is a career diplomat, but in between 'postings', he is a mercenary in the service of Dimitrian (or anyone who might pay more), a General in charge of the United Nations Relief Force, a Consular official, a professional croquet player, sometime Mayor of Binchester, and now, retired, he is Chairman of Binchester Country Club.

It is also rumoured he blew up his laboratory where he worked, and, was forced to go abroad where he became a mercenary, and that is how he got his name.

Today, he is at a meeting of the General Committee of the Binchester Country Club. He has trimmed his moustache a bit more in such a way that it is now a 'pencil' moustache. He is dressed in a smart dark blue blazer, cavalry twill trousers, brogues and a suspect regimental tie. His hair is a bit thinner and the lines on his face more marked. He announces, "I have received a letter from a certain Anatoli Semenov who lives near Binchester. In it, he offers to buy Binchester Country Club for twenty-five million pounds. He says he will demolish the club house, build a new one in its place, extend into the car park while retaining the squash courts, replace the croquet hut with a new brick built one with electricity, buy the neighbouring estate and turn it into a much-needed extended car park. He will grass over two tennis courts and replace them with croquet lawns. In this way, he says he will improve facilities for all members and give an outlet for working croquet players to play in the evening any day of the week. This will promote croquet, an underestimated game."

The committee members are remarkably similar in appearance; suited, always with tie, except Grouch who insists on wearing a bow-tie, always. Their thinning hair betrays their age, their faces lined but their chins broad and square. Collectively they show a statement of intent 'forever'.

On hearing the Chairman's statement, there was a gasp of astonishment, a sharp intake of breath and a sudden shocked silence you could almost touch. No one said anything, until Grouch, the club treasurer, said, "Well, I'll be dammed!"

"I don't believe what I am hearing!" from Scriabin, the secretary.

"Shake me all about!" from the Shaker, the tennis club representative.

"What about my opinion?" said Contract, the Bridge representative (whose opinion was never usually asked).

And from Peta, the croquet representative, "Sounds a good idea!"

The General continued, "Is it your wish I ask our accountants, solicitors and bank managers to assess this offer and if positive, to convene an Extraordinary General Meeting for a vote of the members?"

The members of the committee said that they thought that was a good idea.

After the drama in the boardroom, and anticipating good times ahead, the committee members felt they needed to get away from it all to gather their senses and to recoup. They would go out for the evening to celebrate!

The Four Seasons Hotel and Country Club in Parsley Witney is the social capital of the universe, and was where an evening of skittles was in progress, and where many croquet players had gathered; The Master of Ceremonies, was in full flow. "Roll up, roll up, the Killer's Cup is now beginning. Anyone can take part"

Peta took her shot, bang, bang, bang, along the floor – missed everything. Then Michael, a new member, hits one skittle out of ten, Glam followed 'nil points', Princess Razzle Dazzle – five skittles! Finally, Charles – one skittle. Second Round: Michael misses everything! Razzle Dazzle and Charles, three skittles each. Final Round: Razzle Dazzle nil points, Charles one skittle. He is the winner! He receives a nice bottle of bubbly!

The Binchester Committee members, having watched all this, and deciding the night was as yet young, elected to have some further refreshment and repaired to the Honey Pot in Lasham where the members had an excellent meal with the aid of two to three bottles of wine and a chaser. Feeling replenished, and in high spirits, the quartet decided that since the night was still young and that they were about to be due a windfall from Count Semenov, they unanimously (but they could hardly get the word out) agreed they should return to the Four Seasons again for a nightcap.

Peta, sensing trouble, said she had to go home as Rocky went to bed early, and she did not want to disturb him. The remainder of the members repaired to the tap bar of the Four Seasons, Grouch driving. Arriving safely, they downed another bottle of bubbly and a couple of 'shorts' and a couple of pints of 'best brew'. Declaring they were now feeling absolutely tiptop, and it was now time to return home to their wives, they piled into Grouch's car; unfortunately, instead of taking a right turn out of the hotel, Grouch took a left turn. Contract noticed the error and told Grouch to turn around, which he did, but entered the wharf to the *John Pinkerton*, the canal boat on the Basingstoke canal instead. Missing his bearing, and taking slightly too wide a turn, he very unfortunately drove his car plus occupants over the canal bank and into the muddy waters of the canal. Luckily for him, the water was only two feet six inches deep and all escaped unharmed, but were wet-through, covered in mud, feeling rather decidedly the worse for wear, and leaving the car in the water.

Luckily, someone, a near neighbour, had witnessed what had happened and put a call through to the Emergency Services. It rang in the Mayor's office! The mayor, temporary Mayor Bullock Maclean was out, and the call was taken by his secretary, Frankie, a young female secretary with 'titian' hair culminating in curls hanging down each side of her face, who summoned the police, fire brigade and ambulance. Arriving at the scene, statements were taken from the occupants of the car who were then cautioned and fined on the spot. Points were added to their driving licenses. The fire engines pulled the car out of the water and departed with it to be impounded and collected later by the owners in return for a hefty fee! Seeing no serious injuries, the ambulances departed, but had the grace to call for taxis to take the unfortunate members home to a less than cordial welcome from their wives.

One might wonder where the general was while all this was going on. Wisely, he wasn't there; he had avoided the debacle by having supper at the club, supported by a Drambuie before retiring to bed. The general was a survivor!

It had been twelve months since we had heard from Miss Ballantine, private detective, last seen at 'Best of Show' at Truffles in June 2016. Had she been idle, sipping tea at the tearoom in the Plaza Hotel in Budleigh Salterton? No, sir, she had not! After Truffles, she had fallen to thinking about the way Count Semenov had won the Best of Show dog. How was it he had won so easily, indeed, at the first attempt? Was there something fishy, even *doggie* going on? Had some cash exchanged hands, she wondered? She set herself to make an investigation.

She chose to look at the background of the judges. Did any have a foreign background? How had she been allowed in without a proper search? How had Count Semenov and Peter Mikhail the true pretender got in? Had the porter on the gate been nobbled? Or the attendant in the hall?

She thought she would look firstly at the gate security, and then look at the background of the judges. Being a well-known private detective, she had no need herself to stand outside people's doorways for hours on end, or 'bug' their phone calls, or hack their computers. Anyway, that was illegal. She had a team to probe and investigate other people's lives.

Two weeks later, she had a result. The car park attendant was Ruthuanian, the door attendant also Ruthuanian and one of the judges also Ruthuanian. That was a start. Had they any criminal record? Strangely enough, it transpired that Count

Semenov had been investigated for burglary and embezzlement in the past. The plot thickened. Was there a connection between them?

Miss Ballantine's team had followed one of the security guards to a hotel in Kensington, The Imperial, where he had an interview with Count Semenov. That did not reveal anything, but they had photographic evidence from Truffles, but still it wasn't enough to gain a conviction. Miss Ballantine sought a police warrant to search the rooms of the Count, and the car park attendant, and the Ruthuanian judge, and, hey presto, in each of the rooms was a theatre ticket for the same theatre production of 'He stoops to win'.

Now, to investigate their bank statements to see if any heavy cashflow had happened. Yes, again, five thousand pounds to each of the car park attendants and five hundred thousand pounds to the judge. Where had this sudden inflow of money come from? It was time to hand the case over to the solicitors.

INTERVIEW ROOM AT MESSRS SNODGRASS, INGLEBASHER AND TWOFINGERS.

"Is that so?" murmured Mr Snodgrass. Mr Snodgrass was really past retirement, but had agreed to stay on for this case. He definitely had coiffured hair, a prominent nose and cheeks, which were ruddy, and he concealed a small bottle of something medicinal between some books bookended on his desk.

"Really," he said. And, "You think so?"

"Mmmmm, you don't say,"

"Tut, tut." Then he said again, "Really, we must look into

this."

Then another, "Really, oh dear, oh dear!"

At last, "Really? Most interesting! Dear me, tch, tch, tch. Thank you, Miss Ballantine, Goodbye."

Three months later…

Almost exactly at the same time, three events took place, only separated by the time it takes for communication to take place from one event to the next.

Crown Court, Binchester 6.30pm September 21st 2016

His Justice Lord Spigot was in session. The count perceived him as a thin wiry man with pointed chin and little curls at the top of his head which blended beautifully with the curls of his wig.

"You, Count Semenov, have been accused of perverting the course of justice, bribery and corruption. Do you plead guilty or innocent?"

"Not guilty, my lord."

"Very well then, in view of the severity of the crime, I require that this case be held at the Old Bailey at a time that can be arranged at the earliest opportunity; meanwhile, your passport will be retained; bail will be allowed at one million pounds. Do you understand?"

Count Semenov thought he did and smiled his enigmatic smile.

Boardroom, Binchester Country Club, 6.31pm September 21st, 2016

The general in the chair, General Battlin' Dave said, "Well, gentleman, you have heard that our money has been pulled out from under our feet. Firstly, the twenty-five million pounds promised has only been paid in instalments. When the clubhouse was extended, the count paid the bill in stages. He bought the plot next door for five million pounds; now, we will have to sell it back at a loss and there are contract penalties for non-fulfilment of contract. We will have to knock down the clubhouse extension because we will not have a car park, and that will use any money left over from the sale of the plot. Gentlemen, we will not be able to reduce our subscriptions, indeed, we may have to increase them. The only consolation is that the conversion of the two tennis courts to croquet lawns has not been done. In effect, we are back where we started."

The members were once more stunned into silence.

Groucho exclaimed, "This is outrageous!"

Scriabin gurgled into his beard, "Shocking, shocking!"

"I've never known anything like this!" Contract declared.

The meeting adjourned and the representatives declared they needed a break and would return later. One by one, they adjourned to the Tap Room of the Four Seasons Hotel to drown their sorrows.

Committee Meeting, Binchester Croquet Club,
6.32 pm September 21st, 2016

The chairman's speech had Peta on her feet. "Fellow members; we have heard of the downfall of Count Semenov; but, are we downhearted? No, we are not; we have a new croquet hut so I want to drink a toast to Count Semenov; he was not such a bad fellow after all!"

Notice in the Binchester Herald:

Pedigree Russian wolfhounds for sale; one thousand pounds each.

Best of Show award at Truffles.

Apply to Count Semenov at the Monastery Troitskia, Moscow.

Enquiries to psemenov@pinkyonder.com.

Count Semenov arrived at Popham Airfield near Basingstoke; his plane had been made ready. The Trilander had not been impounded as no one knew about it. The count smiled his enigmatic smile and boarded his plane. Air traffic control gave permission for take-off, the flight plan approved and Count Semenov flew off into the sunset. Maybe he might return to play croquet.

PS. A letter arrived from Peter Mikhail the true pretender to Anatoli the count; it said, *"Dear Anatoli, I am so enjoying my stay here that I am thinking of extending my contract. Mr Tyrinov is still acting as Czar, so I am safer here at present. I will keep in touch though. Ciao!"*

CHAPTER FOUR
The Match

Much as the lawyers tried to spoil the narrative of the tales, this chapter tells of the first plot to overthrow President Tyrinov.

It tells how an unknown sports club such as Binchester Croquet Club was involved, unexpectedly, in 'espionage'; but there it is, that is what happened in 'The Match'. A secret agent, known to me (Charles) by his code name of Christopher, played for Fittleton in this annual Derby between Fittleton and Binchester. In fact, Christopher told me that he had thoroughly enjoyed his time with BI10 and that his specialty was 'lock picking'. Christopher was a short man with hands like a metal crusher; he was both an agent and a courier.

MARCH 2017

The scene: Fittleton Croquet Club. Nice warm weather, flags flying, bunting arrayed round the lawns; tea being served, music discreetly being played. Players in white, tossing for whom to start, how many *bisques* to take, how long should each match take? Central timing – all were to start at the same time: the 'clunk' of croquet ball against mallet, the tinkling of teacups and the hissing of the kettle. All were part of the scene!

The bell rang: Rocky for Binchester, Christopher for Fittleton on lawn one; Glam versus Ivan on lawn two; Peta for the sandwiches; and Josephine for the tea! Play proceeded and chatter continued, mindless of events on the croquet lawn. The score was: Fittleton, one – Binchester, nil. Everything was super – OK. Stories were retold regarding every family's adventures on holiday, and who was speaking to whom and who was not. Score was then Fittleton, one – Binchester, one.

While this was going on, unnoticed, at the corner of the gate to Fittleton, a small man waited; dressed in a postman's uniform, he wanted to speak to the 'guv'nor'. This turned out to be Christopher, who whilst playing, had been waiting for 'a message'. Hurrying to the gate, he received an envelope marked 'the Guv'nor'.

The small man said, "'e didn't say who 'e was, just said, give it to the man with the 'iron handshake'; in there, 'e said."

Christopher opened the envelope; it said:

Go to 123 St Mathew's Road; he will be waiting. Hand over the package. All agents alerted. Operation Nellie is 'go'!

Back to the match: the band struck up a Souza March, *The Stars and Stripes*; cheers echoed round the small ground. Fittleton, two – Binchester, one. Perpetuum had lost to Princess Razzle Dazzle. No surprise there, she was wearing a white dress with coloured frills at the ends of her sleeves and at the bottom of her dress. This had provoked a certain froideur in one section of the crowd and a frisson of excitement in another section depending on one's position in society's gender spectrum. Then, Fittleton, two – Binchester, two. The Analyst had beaten Johnny.

"What a lovely day!" said Aunt Agatha to Charles. "And now we can all go home and put our feet up."

THE COURIERS

All respectable spy agencies insist that agents are not known to each other, which suggests that agents cannot keep a secret; that may be so, but agents are not chosen for their social integrity, but for their stamina under duress. They may have to 'tail' someone for hours, or to stake out a premises for more hours; this requires an ability to stand upright for long periods, and risks being arrested for loitering.

Christopher, courier number one, remembered his training and approached 123 St Mathew's Road cautiously, taking a taxi, then public transport to two blocks beyond the house, and walking past the property two or three times to make sure he was not tailed. He wore a wig and spectacles to further avoid recognition. Quickly, he placed the package through the 'drop' (the letterbox) and departed.

The number two courier's appearance, on picking up the package, was of an unremarkable man, of small stature and build and slightly stooping. He used a walking stick, which sometimes got in the way when he walked, causing him to become unsteady, and make sudden avoiding movements. The most striking part of his demeanor was his eyes, which were constantly roving, as if he was looking for a handhold, or perhaps being followed, even inside his house; more likely, they concealed an enquiring mind, which may well have contributed to his position as a senior agent. Officially retired, he remained on the Secret Service Reserve List as a courier, as indeed, did Christopher.

All BI10 agents have a code name; on this occasion, it would have been impossible for BI10 to name the courier at 123 St Mathew's Road by the name his friends called him, which was Malcolm the Magnificent, so he was simply given the code name of Malcolm Agent X.

Malcolm Agent X needed to call on all his reserves; this was not going to be easy. It was seven years since his last consignment as an expert witness for a Court Tribunal in the trial of a foreign agent, and since then he had become slack and overweight and not exercised as he used to in the gym at the tennis club. He would need to do some emergency exercises, stock up with provisions in case he had to do a 'stake-out' and papers to show who he was not. Money in several currencies were provided for him in the dossier Agent Christopher had left. Then, he would need to take Pepe, his faithful hound – they would take care of each other, wouldn't they?

Malcolm Agent X left his house at five a.m., disguised as a 'suit', hat well down over his left eye; the agency car took him to Northolt Airport, where he took the Queen's flight to Orly Airport, just outside Paris. That was the easy bit. He jumped on the metro to central Paris, got off at Gare du Nord station, and then… the unexpected happened! He got stuck on the escalator going down; his briefcase with incriminating codes was caught in the guard rail and he couldn't dislodge it. People were stacked up behind him, unable to go up or down or to pass him. Malcolm Agent X tugged at the briefcase, but it wouldn't budge. What was he to do? Should he press the panic button supplied to him by the agency, and in effect blow himself up with the suitcase? No! He was a practical man; he removed the screwdriver, chisel and hammer he always travelled with, and systematically unscrewed the briefcase from its handle, exciting the curious, and now amused, and then, admiring glances of the nearest travellers.

"Phew, emergency over!" he gasped to himself, and he said to all around him that he hoped he hadn't spoilt their journey "Merci, pardon!"

Pepe also said, in doggy language, "Phew!"

He had white ends to his ears, so he could be recognised in a crowd.

"Now, for the drop," Agent X said to himself. It was to be in a luggage locker, but which one? He took out his goggles and read '– 969' or was it '696 –'? How could he be sure? Then he remembered there was a 'dash' at the end of the number, so it was '696 –'.

"Phew and phew again!" Now he could go and have a stiff cup of Absinthe in the station restaurant.

Watching this somewhat surreal act, hidden in the shadows behind a pillar in the station, was Agent Y (courier number three).

"This was not how it was supposed to be done," she said. "If I was doing it, I would have done it this way." She proceeded to explain to herself her own system. Agent Y was none other than Dazzler; she was in Paris on her way to meet her counterpart in the twinned town of Malle, near Antwerp.

Agent Y had been recruited in her home town of Parsley Wintney in Hampshire by someone who had come to the door and asked her if she wished to train to be an agent for Aroma Cosmetics, Europe, with free travel and subsistence allowance. She had said to herself, "Well, I am a free agent, so why not?" Unfortunately, she had not known that Aroma Cosmetics was a code name for Foreign Office Operatives, and it was only when she went on a training course, involving obstacle runs, para-gliding and assault techniques, she realised it was not what she imagined. Too late, she had signed the Official Secrets Act!

Anyway, she was intrigued, she was going to Malle, near Antwerp, so, why not collect and then drop off the package as instructed? All travel arrangements had been made, so it was a doddle, and she was being paid. There was one hitch. Unknown to her, but known to all intelligence agencies all over the world, 'sleepers' were placed by the opposition in unspecified and spontaneous locations in case anything of interest might turn up. So, it just happened, she was being observed by Agent A, who, reporting back to his headquarters in Moscow asked, "What should he do?"

"Follow her," he was told; so, he did, one 'suit' following another 'suit.'

Agent Y, blissfully unaware of this sinister development, arrived at her destination town followed by Agent A. Agent Y went to her drop point, a visitor's postbox in the town hall, oblivious to the rather shady gentleman speaking in to his mobile at the previous corner, Agent Z (courier number four).

All drops have to be done at a precise time so that no time is wasted, and everyone knows what he or she has to do and where they have to be. Thus, it was new Agent Z who was in position at the precise time Agent Y did the drop. He had observed Agent A observing Agent Y doing her drop. Agent Z therefore rang his boss in London and asked what he should do.

"Follow him," was the answer. "Then dispose of him," they said this in code, of course, as nothing has to be open and obvious.

Now, you have one guess as to who Agent Z was. Quite right, it was none other than the ubiquitous, Battlin' Dave, a man used to many parts, a known mercenary hiring himself out to well-heeled employers. Battlin' Dave's mission was to take the package to Moscow, where he had many contacts; on this occasion, he was to meet a certain VIP who was the destination for his message. He would not know who he was but the VIP would identify himself.

Agent Z, as we should call him, knew what he had to do. He might be followed, of course, by another Russian agent, or Russian Agent A but he would dispose of him by the very effective method he had witnessed at St Helena some years before: he would skewer him with a croquet hoop on the night train and put the body out of the train. Neat and not obvious.

To avoid recounting indelicate details, Agent Z duly disposed of Agent A on the night train, and on arriving at Moscow Central was met by a distinguished looking man, none other than Count Semenov, of course, his name on his lapel. "Thank you, comrade, I will take possession of this package," he said, and disappeared into the crowd.

A FAILED PLOT, JUNE 2017

All spies are continually reporting to their handlers and back to their headquarters staff to gain an advantage over their competitors. Thus it was, that messages decoded in the Moscow Headquarters deemed there was a plot to assassinate President Tyrinov; press agencies round the world, seeing that the president had not appeared in public for two weeks, had said that dissident Soviet groups were determined to destroy President Tyrinov to gain power for themselves. Western governments, determined to prove that Russia was governed by cabals of Mafia crooks, had put it out that rival gangs of criminals vied to be the first to be nominated for the glory of eliminating the Russian president.

In fact, what had happened was that Operation Nelly, carefully planned and nurtured in the west, had foundered on lack of popular support. Was it a CIA plot, a terrorist coup, even a Whitehall inspired conspiracy? All the western governments denied any involvement and offered President Tyrinov their support at the same time.

The idea behind Operation Nellie was that agents carefully selected and trained in the west, would descend on a whole host of Russian towns and villages, broadcast messages of defiance in the market squares, and on radio, and incite a popular uprising of the people, hoping that they, in their millions, would demand an end to the Russian autocracy but the Russian people had not responded; Russians had full employment even if the jobs might be menial. The exhortations had been a damp squib; however, there had been repercussions. The Russian security services had rounded up the ringleaders and instead of the old Russian punishment of 'fire and knout' had, in fact, fired (razed) the houses of the 'revisionists' to the ground, exiled them to the fastnesses of the Urals and told them to write a twenty-thousand-word essay recanting their sins entitled, *'How NOT to organise a coup'*. Some wag in the Kremlin had made up the title.

THE THEATRE, BANQUET AND BALL, SEPTEMBER 2017

President Tyrinov, after two weeks of lying low, had reappeared and decreed that there should be celebrations in his honour including a Grand Ballet at the Marinsky Theatre, St Petersburg, followed by a banquet and ball in Prince Menshikov's Palace.

It was to be a grand occasion; full regalia and evening dress were expected. The Marinsky Theatre is a fine building inside and outside; stuccoed interior, plush seating, the Czar's box in the centre with the finest view of the enormous proscenium. The stage can be moved in its entirety to one side or the other to allow a full set change.

The invited guests, including ambassadors, dignitaries, foreign princes and heads of state, leaders of commerce, the arts and the sciences had been invited to celebrate the arrest of the leaders of the attempted putsch, and to show Russia's commitment to justice, law and order.

President Tyrinov arrived in a bomber jacket, shaped trousers and pointed shoes and with just one badge pinned to his lapel, the order of Stalin. The president had not served in any campaigns. Count Semenov arrived festooned with medals from top to bottom; there were so many orders of chivalry in Russian society that everyone could boast at least half a dozen medals. Upset by this brazen show of metalwork, the president took Count Semenov aside and said to him, "You are walking a fine line, *mon ami;* you took in the real Pretender Peter Czarevitch as your guest and were the last person to see him. He is a wanted man. You can perhaps tell us where he is – otherwise, it will be difficult for you carrying all these baubles!"

"Of course, comrade; the last time I saw him was one year ago, when I asked him to look after my dogs in my estate in Hampshire," replied the count.

"We have looked there, and he is not there, so, where is

he? I am asking you to find him," said the president, self-styled 'real Czar', as the curtain rose for the opera-ballet.

The opera, as it turned out to be, was set to a background of the Russian interior, forests, rivers and mountains; a full orchestra played a mighty introduction, actors appeared in a variety of poses, blacksmiths hammering, labourers labouring, a horse and rider appeared, a messenger fled across the stage bearing news of a public spectacle; scenes were enacted of a traditional punishment, the brutal 'knout', a whip three and a half feet long that would tear strips off a victim's back. Bases and baritones strutted across the stage. It was all very dramatic, a message to anyone who might think they could question the established authority of the state could get away with it would be mistaken!

After this spectacle, everyone claiming to be exhausted, nevertheless, repaired to Prince Menshikov's grand palace for a great feast; and what a palace! Built on the banks of the River Neva in Peter the Great's time in 1705, it was in the best Italian style, bigger and better than Peter the Great's modest one-storied, three-roomed log chalet. Peter the Great enjoyed having big functions there, but preferred a simpler lifestyle himself.

Menshikov's stone palace was three stories high with ornate iron plates on the roof painted red; it had a spacious main hall for banquets with elegant furniture, silver service and ornate candelabras, damask furnishings fit for a Czar.

Feasts were still in the grand style of the 1700s and 1800s *a la Russe;* many toasts were drunk, courses were plenty, food – a vast array of different dishes. Russians did not consider that civilities had been satisfied unless guests were completely incapable of moving afterwards. Accordingly, guests frequently went to sleep where they sat and the ball with suitable entertainment afterwards never took place!

President Tyrinov, President of all Russia, Chairman of the Supreme Soviet Congress, chairman of this, that and every committee, father of the people, autocrat, was, however, a worried man; not that the worry was overwhelming, he was used to that, but that it was just there, like a mote in the eye, a floater that moved around, but stayed there, like a tiny cloud in the distance that seemed to get bigger, but remained the same distance away.

The cause of his worry was none other than his rival, the real pretender, Peter Mikhail Czarevitch; where was he? That was what he could not comprehend. In Old Russia, to have a rival was to have a 'death sentence' over one's head. Contenders for the throne plotted, and where there was one, there would be others. That was his worry; he could not sleep and that was a worry too.

In his mind's eye, Vladimir thought of Peter the Pretender as someone he could get on with, like himself, magnanimous but all powerful. He could not take that liberty. Vladimir then imagined Peter as sitting on an upturned crate, playing chess with a friend on an old oil drum somewhere in the world, but where?

Count Semenov was the key; he was the last person to see Peter Mikhail Czarevitch. The pretender was factotum to the Russian wolfhound stud in Old Hampshire, England, but when this lead was investigated, it went cold. He could not apprehend Anatoli Semenov as he was the only contact. Yes, he had him trailed; every avenue explored. There would be contact between Anatoli and Peter sooner or later, and then he would have him.

Vladimir smiled smugly but also grimly. What would

happen if there was a popular uprising against him? He would be sacked, dragged through the streets of Moscow on the end of a pole or worse, confined to peeling potatoes for the rest of his life in Siberia!

NOVEMBER 2017

Somewhere out there, the real pretender was doing what the self-styled Czar Vladimir was thinking; Peter Mikhail Czarevitch was sitting on an upturned crate playing chess on an oil drum with a friend. He had been promoted; he was now Sergeant Michel of the French Foreign Legion posted to any area of crisis where there was French influence. Now he was in the Pacific Islands of Samoa where there had been a major cyclone, helping Médecins Sans Frontières with the rescue and restoration work.

Suddenly, there was a call from the commandant's office. "Would Sergeant Michel come quickly to the office as there was an urgent message for him?"

"Sit down, Michel," said the commandant. "You are requested by your controller to go immediately to Oslo; here are your papers. Report to exit control at 07.00 hours. That is all."

So, Sergeant Michel, now Peter Mikhail the true pretender, arrived in Oslo being met by his controller, Colonel Rich. "You are now to become better known," he said. "You are to become a Consular Official with the Swedish Embassy in St Petersburg. You will be quite safe; you cannot be arrested on foreign soil!"

So it was, that Peter was to meet face to face with Russian citizens seeking a better life in the west; also, meeting some of Vladimir's agents, who reporting back to their master, announced that almost certainly Peter the Pretender was now an embassy official, and, more ominously, preparing to make his move.

Before Vladimir could make any constructive restrictive orders, Peter was moved again by his controller, Colonel Rich, this time to the French embassy in London performing the same duties. One day, the controller said to Peter that they would take the day off to go to Binchester to see how the Russian wolfhounds were doing. They arrived late one morning; knowing they would be shadowed by one of Vladimir's agents.

"We will lead him a dance," the controller said.

At the stud, they were greeted by the out-house staff, Stan, and overlooking the wall to the estate, was a reporter for the Daily Echo or so he said he was, but he was one of Vladimir's agents, who reporting back to Moscow, said, "We have him now; he cannot escape. We will pick him up at dawn, and then you may have your will!"

So it seemed, but Peter and the controller had other ideas. Using the secret underground tunnel that many old country properties had built in case of attack in the English Civil War of the 1600s, they made their escape to a waiting Bentley limousine and back to the French Embassy. "We have led them a pretty dance!" the controller said.

Back in Moscow, an incandescent Vladimir had a kind of fit, "You have let them escape again; you will pay for this!"

And so, dear reader, who is to be the winner in this game of 'top dog' between Vladimir, the self-styled Czar, and Peter Mikhail, the true pretender? Also, who did the insignificant little man at the gate to Fittleton Croquet Club receive his orders from? Who was the mysterious Colonel Rich? Find out, perhaps, in the next chapter.

CHAPTER FIVE
The Challenge!
January 2018

Sergeant Michel was popular amongst his men and superiors; he could change a plug, mend a fuse, change a light bulb, put up a shelf, repair a window or door frame, but above all, he was able to make a temporary home for the people of the devastated island of Voorayamy with palm leaves supported by wooden frames, and at a rate of ten homes daily, he was voted 'worker of the month'. He also made model boats like his illustrious forebear, Peter the Great.

When he got home from the French Embassy in London, waiting for him was his controller, Colonel Rich, a shadowy kind of figure, a bit like General Battlin' Dave, a man with connections to Count Semenov. Seconded to the French Foreign Legion, he had emigrated from Salisbury, England, one year previously. Rich had been in 'business' before, but what kind of business was not something people asked about! Now he was Peter's handler. Soon, they were playing chess.

"P to Q two," Colonel Rich said, as he sat on an upturned crate facing Peter.

"OK, then I move R to B eight and check," responded Peter.

They were in Voorayamy, far from prying Russian spies. The Foreign Legion had kept Rich's rank. "Now, Peter, we must have a better plan next time. 'Nellie' didn't work, because the people did not see you. It makes all the difference! Our agents are still in place, though some were rounded up and sent to Vladivostok. We will call this plan 'Nellie Two'."

"Sounds good," Peter said. "How do we start?"

"Well, what we do is to announce to the people that an important person is due to appear and give a speech. This, we will do in all the towns and villages, as we did last time. The essence of this plan is speed. We will be in and out before the authorities have a chance to catch up with you, and we will be at our next venue before they can catch a cold."

"Well, it is bold, but might just work," Sergeant Michel said.

While the two conspirators were working on their plan, news came in from the Reuters News Agency of a dispatch from a Russian News Agency that a foreign spy had been banished from Russian territory. It read as follows:

A British Consular Official has been sent home for undiplomatic behaviour. His name is General Battlin' Dave. It appears that on the morning of the 29th January 2018, a lorry loaded with chemicals exploded outside where he was staying. On one of the canisters was an etched caption which read 'Made in Reading, England'. Our gallant agents linked this incident to the general when he appeared in a distraught state at the bottom of his staircase shouting, 'Why me? Why me?' he was traced to the British Embassy, and assurance was given he worked there. He was instantly dismissed and given one hour to pack his bags." End of bulletin.

A later report from the British Embassy read:

General Battlin' Dave has returned to England after the end of his elected contract. A medical report has recommended immediate retiral. The general retires after many years of distinguished service.

A further report in the Hampshire Chronicle read:

General Battlin' Dave has retired to an Old Officer's Home near Binchester. He had been seen at several elderly soldier's reviews wearing all his medals, but without his pistol at his side!

"The general has finally got his marching orders then," said Colonel Rich.

"I guess you're right," replied Sergeant Michel.

COUNT SEMENOV AT BAY FEBRUARY 2018

Many revolutionaries make the mistake of fighting with their comrades only to get killed, captured or disabled in some way. With their demise, dies a dream; the inspiration and ideas behind the movement are no longer there to guide or inspire the revolutionaries to further heights of daring and maybe even effectiveness.

This was not the case with Count Semenov; he had returned home from the private airfield outside Moscow for a change of clothing and a rest and reappraisal of the plans for the next stage for the return of the true Czar. These were dangerous times. Count Semenov was the prime target for information on this putative Czar. Insiders in the Kremlin knew that an assault on the Russian Presidency was imminent; it was paramount to find 'leads' to this imminent putsch.

Vladimir Tyrinov was nervous, so were his henchmen; failure was equivalent to a lifetime's exile in Siberia! "Any news?" he asked of Yuri Bonetski.

"No, none, comrade," Yuri replied.

"May heaven spare me from incompetent fools!" Vladimir railed. Such was the mood in the Kremlin!

Count Semenov was leading a double life. Caught up in a court case in England, his every step followed in Russia, it seemed the only safe place for him was in the air. Thus, it was, that he had soon taken off again, and was high up in the sky enjoying his blinis and smoked salmon; his islander jet was passing over the English coastline at thirty-two thousand feet. "We have contact with Popham, my count," said the co-pilot.

"Good, then commence your landing procedures," the count replied.

Five minutes later, they touched down on the airfield. There were no immigration or customs process, which might have been expected to rouse some curiosity, since he had come from Russia. The truth was that Count Semenov had filed a flight plan from Islederney. No one was going to check that. It was far too mundane.

Waiting for them at his country house near Binchester were his housekeeper, his gardener and keeper of hounds, Stan.

"Welcome home, sire; all is ready."

"Good, then we do not have a moment to lose," Count Semenov said. "The Russian FSB are after us; they will surely catch on sooner or later, even though they are fools".

The next morning was Monday, February 28th 2018. After breakfast, Count Semenov said, "Send out the signal for the start of Operation Nellie Two!"

A few days later, while out jogging in the park, Count Semenov felt suddenly faint. Gasping for air, he collapsed and died before any attempts could be made to revive him.

At an inquest a few days later, a jury found an open verdict; death by misadventure, no known cause. No suspicious circumstance was noted, but samples were sent for analysis for toxicology to specialist laboratories around the world. Could it be poisoning? There were no signs of a struggle or injury and all organs were normal. The Russians were world leaders in toxicology; there had been assassinations before linked to a poisoned umbrella tip. This could be another.

A few weeks later, a report appeared in the national newspapers that a Botany Professor at the Royal Physics Gardens had detected a trace of Gelsemium in samples sent for analysis. This did not prove anything but Gelsemium is a highly poisonous plant.

It is an evergreen climber with white flowers common in the Northern USA; related to Jasmine, it contains highly toxic alkaloids which if taken in sufficient dose produce an effect similar to Strychnine, paralysis of muscles, inability to breathe and death following quickly; it is also used in homeopathy to produce a calming effect.

It will be noted that Aunt Agatha takes Gelsemium as a homeopathic cure; as yet there have been no untoward adverse effects.

INVASION! MARCH 2018

The scene was set: the challenge set in motion. It could not be stopped. The order had been given from a source impossible to trace. Count Semenov was dead. Therefore, he could not countermand it!

In theory, the attackers had an advantage; Moscow could not know from where they would attack. However, they did know a lot. There had been activity in the Northern Russian seas, north and to the east of Archangel; also, activity had been noticed in the seas to the east of Russia, between Russia and Japan and also in the Baltic Sea. Schooners, five of them, had been seen exercising in each of these areas; helicopter activity had been observed between the schooners. More recently, similar activity had been noticed in the Caspian and Black seas. Whatever was happening was going to use helicopters. So much, so good! Right, so far! That was as much, however, as the FSB could determine.

Colonel Rich was in charge of the exercises going on in the various locations mentioned. The exercises went on all week rehearsing the tactics. Helicopter A would fly from Base A1 to Base C1; helicopter B would fly from Base B1 to D1 and so on around the area. At the same time, helicopter AA would fly from Base A1 to Township T1, helicopter BB would fly from Base B1 to Township T2, helicopter FF would fly from Base F1 to Township T6 and so on. It was meticulously organised to cause the greatest uncertainty in the defending forces despite their overwhelming firepower.

Colonel Rich's helicopters were only lightly armed for self-defence and to give the helicopters maximum range.

On one of these exercises, the true pretender flew along to understand the procedure and practice for his role, which was to make a short speech to the townsfolk of the town he was dropped at. He would be there no longer than ten minutes, before being airborne again and it was hoped that by so doing, he would be able to convince the population that he was the true Czarevitch, and that they, the people, would rise up in their hundreds and thousands and demand that Russia have a Czar again.

That was the hope, anyway! If it did not work, they were in trouble! However, everyone who had been in contact with Peter Mikhail knew he was the true descendent of the last Czar and the Russian people were a conservative people.

Day one and the challenge began at nine a.m. promptly. In a bewildering display of precision, all helicopters took off as planned crisscrossing over Russia; owing to a limit of five hundred miles each way that the helicopters could travel, they could only visit townships within this range. Peter made a short speech at each stop, gathering interested and curious people each time. His immense height gave credence to his story, as Czar Peter the Great had been six feet seven inches tall. He also had documents on him to show he was the true descendent of Czar Ussuri.

The FSB chief was baffled. Every time his spotters saw the true pretender in one of the townships, by the time his troops got there, he was gone! And what was worse was the fact that the crowds were growing. Even if Peter wasn't there, the crowds gathered in case they might spot him. It was like looking for a needle in a haystack. Peter's speech was short. Usually he said, "I am the true Czar; look at me. Peter the Great was even taller, and I am nearly as tall! Do you want your Czar back? You can have proof. The FSB know I am related to Czar Ussuri. They just don't want the old days back. I am not looking to rule Russia, only to act as its soul and spiritual leader."

It was sufficient. The crowd loved it; it was what they wanted to hear. President Tyrinov in the Kremlin was incensed. Why couldn't the fools find him? Someone's head would roll. His ulcer begun to gnaw at him; he began to feel sick and faint. "Fetch me my Kalashnikov and my Gaviscon and I will find him myself!" he shouted. Such was the desperation in the Russian leader's mind.

Then, suddenly, out of the blue, an unusual incident occurred. A small cadre of Russian soldiers were conducting an exercise in neighbouring fields, when they heard the sound of an approaching helicopter overhead. Running to see what was happening, they saw several hundred people lining the town square. When the helicopter landed, a tall man emerged accompanied by several other people. He, the tall man, started to harangue the people saying he was the true Czar.

The sergeant in charge exclaimed, "He must be mad; we should take him to the nearest police station."

They surrounded the helicopter, shouting, "You are under arrest: lay down any arms you may have!"

The true pretender said he knew that this was what would happen, and welcomed it. "No resistance now, comrades, this is our chance with destiny."

However, instead of being taken to the nearest Political Commissar, they were rather roughly led to the nearest Police Station, and from there, were driven to the nearest psychiatric hospital. The officer in the police station, the station commander, said, "This fellow is obviously mad if he thinks he is the Czar!"

Arriving at the psychiatric hospital, Peter was led into the doctor's interview room. "So, they are saying that you are saying that you are the Czar. What evidence have you of that?"

Unfortunately, all Peter's documents had been removed when he was searched, so he was unable to prove who he was.

"All right then, you cannot prove who you are, then we will give you some 'truth serum' and perhaps that will jog your memory."

Unable to prove who he was, Peter was led to the ward and the door locked tight.

The next day, Peter was taken to the treatment room and given a small dose of an intravenous sedative; he was then asked who he was or who he thought he was. After a while, Peter, dopey under the sedation, replied he was Sergeant Michel.

"Sergeant Michel?" replied the interrogator. "First you are the Czar, and now you are Sergeant Michel! Who is he then? And where does he come from and who does he work for?"

All these questions, thought Peter. *What does it matter? They will do as they please anyway.* "I am Sergeant Michel and I work for the French Foreign Legion."

"Aha; it is as I thought. He is a spy. Now, we will hand him over to the FSB and he will be lucky to get twenty years in Siberia! And I will get a well-deserved promotion and pay rise!" thought the Interrogator, as he promptly filed a report to the local FSB.

It was fortunate that the sergeant in charge of the party that arrested Peter had filed a report to his Station commander and that this report was seen by a young, sharp-eyed clerk; otherwise, it would have been filed away and lost forever. This young man also kept an eye out for circulars coming out of the Kremlin and had noted that an order had been issued for a fugitive male claiming to be the true Czar, that he would be arriving at a Russian town in a helicopter and that he was to be handed over to the FSB. Finding this report on the station commander's desk, he brought it to his attention, together with the Kremlin circular It also so happened that the report sent to the FSB office from the hospital had been sent to a different FSB office and this would never had been noticed unless the young clerk had rung around the local FSB offices to see if there was any other information coming in. The young clerk handed this also to the station commander.

The station commander, the officer in charge, was furious. "As if we do not have enough work to do! Here you are telling me about an imposter claiming to be the Czar! There must be one hundred of them in Russia!" he said to the young clerk, the one to be destined for promotion, not the interrogator at the psychiatric hospital "You go and find all the bogus Czars and bring them to me, and I will notify our president"

The young clerk collected fifty-two claimants to be Czar from all the mental institutions in Russia; the Kremlin was notified, and the Kremlin demanded they be brought for an identity parade before President Tyrinov.

IDENTIFICATION! JULY 2018

Thus it was, that fifty-two putative Czars were paraded before President Tyrinov. The President quickly identified the six feet five inches, Peter. He was also not amused, feeling sick and mad, that it had taken three months before the authorities had been able to produce the true pretender from the time he had been arrested, to the time they brought him in front of the president, the self-styled 'real Czar.'

Vladimir disposed of the remaining imposters and speaking to the guards asked that Peter be given a bath and new set of clothes and then brought before him. When Peter finally arrived, Vladimir said to him, "Well, what are we to do with you? The people want you to be Czar. We know you are the true heir to Czar Nicholas II, but you know what happened to him! Czar Ussuri was an imposter."

"I certainly do," Peter the true pretender said. "You may have your will with me, but then what will the people do with you, I wonder?" Peter replied.

"I will make an offer for you," Vladimir said. "You can be Czar, but you will have no power! You will do as I say. Any deviation, and you will suffer the full consequences of the state. You will have ceremonial duties only. You will welcome Heads of State and Ambassadors, etc.; you can preside at state functions and dinners. You will have an emolument decided by the state. You will take up residence at the Peterhof Palace in St Petersburg and the Grand Palace in Moscow. You will have a staff of ten, not including a cook, doctor and secretary. At all times, if you wish to leave the country, it will by our decree only. Do you understand and do you agree?"

"Yes, I understand, and agree with your proposals," Peter replied.

The significance of the year, 2018, and date, July 16th, was not lost on both men, it was exactly one hundred years to the day since the other Czar, Czar Nicholas II, and his family were assassinated in far off Ekaterinburg. Their remains had been since removed and reinterred in the Peter and Paul Cathedral, St Petersburg in 2008.

And so, in this atmosphere of peace and light, our dream fantasy story ends. Sergeant Michel, formerly of the French Foreign Legion and newly appointed Czar Peter Mikhail of Russia, fades away from the imagination. Michael, serial winner of croquet tournaments, comes to with a start after what has seemed to be a very long night. He wonders, still feeling rather dazed, "Was he really a Czar or just an ordinary star?"

Whatever, his senses returned; he picks up the phone, rings the secretary, and says, "Can you fill in for the next match? I have been let down!"

Tranquillity, harmony and joyfulness descended once again on this small little croquet club of Binchester and we hear the chink of Pimm's filled glasses and the reassuring clunk of a croquet mallet against a croquet ball.

CHAPTER SIX
The Fall and Rise of Binchester CC
Spring 2018 – Summer 2018

While the international situation in the Far East was unsettled and liable to deteriorate, the National Croquet Union was involved in a spat with the National Press.

The imminent demise of croquet was at the back of the Croquet Union's mind. The union was seized with panic. It moaned that, "Without young people coming into the game, croquet will surely be confined to the history books in thirty years' time."

What was to be done? Committees up and down the land devised schemes to offer free croquet, open days, leaflets to be put into public libraries, doctors' surgeries, sports halls, on village notice boards, flyers through letter boxes, in pubs, anywhere where they might be seen and actually looked at.

In desperation, the Croquet Union thought vertically and laterally, any direction at all. They opened themselves up to the gaze of the great British public. Finally, they announced a UK Croquet Day. In a blaze of muted trumpets and damp phrases, The UK Croquet Day was promulgated to be on Sunday June

5th, 2018. The National Union would release a series of press releases on the theme of 'The Croquet Evidence' with a number of template stories that would arouse interest in croquet, and invite clubs to coincide their events with the UK Croquet Day.

The general public tends to think of croquet as a 'pleasant summer garden game'. Predictably, the National Press had a view too and that was uncomplimentary. The Daily Echo screeched:

Croquet is an effete game played by elderly gents with time on their hands.

The Daily Guardian thundered:

Croquet is still a game played on vicarage lawns with glasses of Pimm; it does not deserve print space.

The Daily Telegram was equally dismissive:

Its demise is long overdue; arcane rules and incomprehensibility will surely hasten its departure from the scene.

Indeed, a survey of a snapshot of one thousand shoppers outside Tesco found the majority had heard of Real Frisbee but had not heard of croquet. The national mood was 'not for turning'.

Shades of 'Alice through the Looking Glass', said Charles, sipping his Malt.

Aunt Agatha agreed, "What are we to do with you if you can't play croquet?"

"Well, there's always writing short stories," he said.

Meanwhile, there were rumblings at the next meeting of the main club; Johnny had been summoned to hear the discontent of the policy group which had formed to discuss the future of the club including croquet; the chairman,

Mr Shortsighted, who had taken over from General Battlin' Dave who had retired, had asked the new chair of the policy group, Ms Knowall, to present her views. Ms Knowall was unknown to Johnny. After employment at the Office for Civil Liberties and as Chairwoman of the Association of Teachers Inclusion Committee, she had now been elected as Chairperson of the Policy Group at Binchester Country Club. "Ah ha!" she cried to herself. "Virgin territory. Time for a shake-up!"

Johnny considered her carefully. An initial impression was not very revealing. She was dressed tidily, if unflashily, in a severe grey suit (jacket, trousers and tie). Her hair was turning grey, tied back; her nose was slightly upturned at the end, her lips full and her teeth slightly protruding. Not a lot to go on.

"Well, as you know, Mr Shortsighted, we should consider whether the croquet section is viable. What do you say, Mr Croquet representative? I would like you to come back in one month's time with your answer."

Johnny was not suitably pleased when he reported the mood of the main club to the next subcommittee meeting of the Croquet CC. "I have never been spoken to like this before," he lamented. The Analyst asked the secretary for her report. She was a sparky lady, you could tell by the flashes of light at the end of her sentences!

"Mr Chairman," the secretary said. "We have lost ten members, four died, three moved away and two said they were too indisposed to continue."

"Well then, what are we to do?" the chairman said.

"It is the UK Croquet Day on June 5th. Every time we have an open day, no one turns up!"

The secretary, Glam, added, "What about a crazy croquet

day – all dressed up in Edwardian clothes?"

"Well, er, yes, that is an idea we could live without… I mean, an idea we could consider!" exclaimed The Analyst.

THE UK CROQUET DAY, JUNE 5th, 2018

The day of the Great UK Croquet Day dawned fine; everyone was in fairly good spirits. The secretary had put in details of the UK Croquet day at Binchester CC to the Hampshire Gazette. Free croquet was offered to anyone turning up; all equipment would be provided. All anyone needed was a pair of flat soled shoes. There would be coaching from expert staff. Refreshments were available in the main club restaurant. All that was needed was for members of the public to turn up. Waiting to greet them were two members dressed in Edwardian clothes (Glam and Dazzler); they were to escort the public to the croquet lawns, where they would be handed over to the coaches.

The first arrival was a mother and her teenaged son. "Do you have a junior section?" she asked.

"No, we don't," they said.

Next up was a middle-aged woman in a wheelchair, "Do you take disabled wheelchair users?" she asked.

"No, we don't," they said.

After that, a student arrived with a notepad. "Do you have a gender, race discrimination policy?" he asked.

"No, we don't," they said.

Lastly, a counsellor from Binchester City Council arrived. "Do you have a child protection policy?" he asked.

"Possibly, we are not sure," they said.

There was one nice man with a dog who wanted to join.

"Unfortunately," they said. "We don't take dogs."

Then, emerging from the pavilion, having come through the café-bar, there came three, four, five, no, six figures (were they soldiers?) dressed entirely in white, mallets or rifles slung purposefully over their shoulders, with Norwegian walking sticks in front of them, marching in perfect echelon formation. Who were they? They marched down to the croquet lawns, grim-faced, looking straight ahead, with loping gait across the lawns, interrupting the proceedings, into the hut. There, they exchanged weapons for mallets, and took up position on the corners of the lawns, four to play *Golf Croquet,* and two to play *Association Croquet.* This was a croquet demonstration not a military exercise.

Meanwhile, however, up at the café-bar, pandemonium reigned! Terrified patrons cowered under the tables; someone had popped a champagne cork! The bar attendant had pushed the panic button. The manager had called the mayor's office. 'Bulldog' Maclean was twiddling with his pencil. "It's boring here; there have been no murders today, Frankie," he said. "Where I come from – Newmarket, New Jersey, we have two or three, daily!"

Then he heard, "Send help quickly," from a voice in the café-bar; "someone's been shot; maybe more; it may be a terrorist attack: some dozen or more men heavily-armed are shooting, indiscriminately."

Bulldog readied his pencil. "OK, Buddy, how many casualties?"

No, he couldn't say how many casualties there were; a panicked voice from the croquet club collapsed into a monosyllabic babble. Bulldog Maclean was not one for idling around! Within five to ten minutes, the place was alive with armed police and patrol cars; army tanks had taken up position; a helicopter was circling overhead. The press was alerted of an incident in Binchester. News bulletins were interrupted with developing news: *Casualties at Binchester, several dead, many wounded.*

The officer in command burst into the manager's office, "Where are the terrorists?" he demanded.

A red-faced manager had to say there were no terrorists, only a bunch of croquet players dressed in white.

"This is intolerable; the second time in six months you have called us out on a false emergency. You will hear more from our Chief Constable!" he shouted.

A month later, an envelope dropped into the manager's office. It read:

FINE: for unnecessary call-out of police, army and Air Force: fifty thousand pounds. Payment on receipt of notice.

After the debacle of the mock terrorist invasion, the manager had been removed by the committee to a position of cleaning of municipal facilities in Kyrgyzstan; from there he was not heard of again!

However, things were still not rosy at Binchester CC. At the next *mixin*, four members arrived using walking aids, two of whom had artificial legs. Another four said they had hospital appointments that morning and did not know whether they could come again. A ninth member said he had got the days mixed up, and thought it was Thursday instead of Monday, and a tenth arrived, one and a half hours late; his bus was delayed, he said, due to the time taken for other elderly passengers to get off and on. That left only three relatively fit members, Analyst, Perpetuum and Peta; General Battlin' Dave who although now in a rest home was still eager in spirit but feeling his age came, the Secretary, Malcolm the Magnificent, and Johnny.

At tea afterwards, The Analyst said, "What are we to do? We can barely put out a team now and have had to withdraw from the *League*!"

"Why don't we advertise, not here in this country, but abroad?" Perpetuum said.

The secretary thought this an idea going nowhere. Peta thought it, "ridiculous," and Rocky concurred.

Malcolm the Magnificent, harrumphed and Johnny said nothing and spluttered into his tea.

Perpetuum, said that he was going to put in one advert to a remote mining township in the middle of Nigeria that he had visited as part of his job. "We won't offer him or her any money, only a way of life out of poverty, and I personally will offer whoever it is a year's free board and lodging."

Another meeting of the main club swiftly followed the first. Ms Knowall moved that a vote be taken on the main item on the agenda. "That this club seeing no further use of the croquet section, it being outdated and non-inclusive, moves that it be disbanded and bowls instituted instead."

The motion was carried by eleven votes to one.

ELSEWHERE

In the middle of nowhere, on a sunbaked patch of grass and dirt sat a small boy, aged about ten or eleven years, playing with a stick and some stones. At one point, he had set two sticks upright and was hitting small stones through them with another stick that he had fashioned in the shape of a club. He would sometimes stand upright, and with the stick between his legs hit the stone this way; at other times, he would stand sideways, and hit the stone the other way, as if deciding which was the better way of the two to do it. At another time, he would set the sticks further apart, and see if he could hit the stones through them from further away. If he was standing upright and hitting the stones with the stick between his legs, he would realise that the club would have to be fashioned in a different way; he had made several clubs which were different from the club he would use if he hit the stone from a sideways position. The club he would use if hitting with it between his legs had a projection at a different angle, facing him, in contrast to the other one which faced away from him.

"Mabayoje, come and get your supper; playing your funny games will not keep your supper warm!" cried his mother, Abayomi.

"All right, Mum," he answered. "I'll just finish this game though."

"Come along then, Mabayoje, I have something to tell you. You are going to England! We have won a free year's lodging with a family called Perpetuum!" said his father, Umuru Obasanjo.

Meanwhile, in another part of the world, another small boy was honing up on his playing instincts; in a refugee camp on the borders of Syria and Jordan, having fled the war in neighbouring Syria, a group of small boys were aiming stones at a post set in the ground; one of them took up a stick and started hitting a stone into a gap between two other stones.

"Gee, Mohammed, that is good," said his friend, Mustapha.

"Then, I shall teach you how to do it," Mohammed replied. After two weeks, they were both quite proficient and the envy of their pals.

A week later, an aid worker arrived. "Well, Mohammed," she said. "You are going on a trip with your parents to England. Your parents have been granted asylum. It will be your turn next, Mustapha."

Another three thousand miles away, a young girl was seen hitting another type of ball between two posts. This was Buenos Aires, Polo and Croquet Club. Her name was Jeannie, and she was playing croquet. Her father Johnnie had sent her a message, "Good News, you will be going to England for two to three years. Isn't it exciting?"

On June 21st, 2018, three planes arrived at about the same time at three different airports in England. The first of these, a Pan Am Jumbo from Buenas Aires was met by Johnny.

"Welcome to cloudy, wet England," Johnny said to Jeannie. "You will all be coming home with me and then we will be going to Binchester Croquet Club to see how good you are."

On another plane, a Boeing 727 from Lagos Airport, Nigeria, arrived a small boy and his father; this was Mabayoje and Umuru Obasanjo. They were met by Perpetuum.

"Welcome to rainy England. You will be coming home with me to Southampton, Hampshire, and the first thing we will do is to go to Binchester Croquet Club, where I am resident professional."

Lastly, on an Airbus 327, came Mohammed and his father and mother; they were met by a Mrs Dotty of St Mathew's Road, Binchester. Mrs Dotty kept a guest house and was a chatelaine for Refugees from War Zones.

"Welcome to cold, chilly England," she said. "You will be coming home with me to Binchester, and I will introduce you to Malcolm the Magnificent, who is my neighbour, and who plays croquet at Binchester Croquet Club, and we will be going straight there to meet him."

And that is how they all met by a strange coincidence at the same time, at the same place!

After a while, when they had all been introduced to each other, and played a game or two, it became apparent each of the newcomers was a natural player. Perpetuum, became their spokesman, coach and leader of the first junior section that Binchester Croquet Club had ever known. To make up a team of four, Perpetuum rang the mother of the teenage boy who had come to the open day and said to her that Binchester now had a junior section and would she like her boy to join. She said she would consider it.

Later, her husband rang back. "Of course," he said. "His name is Mathias, Matty, for short."

"That's great then," Perpetuum replied. "We have junior coaching on Mondays, Wednesdays and Fridays with extra coaching on Tuesdays, Thursdays and Bank Holidays."

Perpetuum had several short videos of the essentials of play which he showed the boys and Jeannie and which they then practiced. So quick was their progress that he entered them for a school's tournament and they thrashed the opposition!

Thus, the three boys Mabayoje, Mohammed and Matty, and one girl, Jeannie, set new standards of play for their age group and soon began to get the attention of their elders.

"Come and play with us," they exclaimed. "You are good enough to have an adult's handicap."

At the *mixins*, when members meet to play *Golf Croquet* and *Association Croquet*, they soon began to show their skills.

Peta, the handicapper reduced their handicaps to twenty-two from twenty-four, the top handicap, then twenty, then eighteen and so on until she reached twelve. "I can go no further. Now you will have to see the Regional Handicapper; but first of all, you will have to enter their competitions. There is one on July 15th."

This was a *Golf Croquet Handicap* tournament at Great Damptworth-on-Sea; there were sixteen contestants along with Mabayoje, Mohammed, Jeannie and Matty. The tournament would be played over two days with six matches each day; if a player won their group, they would be in the knockout stages. At the end of the first day, Mabayoje was unbeaten and Mohammed and Matty had five wins out of six, Jeannie had four wins. They were all in the knockout stages. On the second day, Mabayoje won his first two games as did the others so they were in the semi-finals. Mabayoje won comfortably, as did Mohammed, and they would meet in the final; Matty and Jeannie were knocked out at this point. Mabayoje won his final, so Mohammed came second, and Matty and Jeannie came fifth and sixth, respectively.

"And now," said Perpetuum. "For a real test, I am entering you all in the Wiltshire Open. Here you will meet players from all over the region!" This was an *Association Croquet* competition. "Your handicaps will be of no value here, as it is *'level'* play, and handicaps are not used," he said.

Again, on the day, Mabayoje won all his singles matches, as did Mohammed. Matty won four out of five and Jeannie three out of five. On the second day, Mabayoje was unbeatable and won the competition, Mohammed came in third and Matty and Jeannie, fifth and sixth, respectively.

After that, things were never the same again. Their

achievements were mentioned in the Croquet Gazette. The news of the young teenage geniuses found its way into the Hampshire Chronicle:

Young Savvy croquet players hit the jackpot!

None of the new young blood was more than fifteen years of age, indeed, they were from ten to fourteen years old! A flurry of applicants to Binchester Croquet Club followed. Its junior section was the envy of the county. A waiting list had to be imposed. Numbers rose to sixty and then seventy. The chairman was delirious!

An extraordinary meeting of the main club, convened to consider the proposal of the policy group of the main club to disband the croquet section, was dismissed by three hundred and thirty-eight votes to one, the one being Ms Knowall.

Next day, an excerpt from the Daily Thunderer read: *Young geniuses at work on the croquet lawn.*

The Daily Echo said:

I knew it all along: croquet is for everyone!

The Daily Guardian spoke of:

Young morality saved on the croquet lawn!

The Everyday Times ate humble pie:

We got it wrong! They backtracked. *Croquet is for all!*

Charles said, "That was a narrow squeak; how are you doing with Sudoku?"

Aunt Agatha said, "Fine, now that's over. How are you doing with the crossword?"

CHAPTER SEVEN
The Case of the Missing Goblet

With the international and national situations still being unsettled, local events were also going downhill. 'Dysfunctional' was a word being used by the cognoscenti.

A longstanding member of Binchester Croquet Club was used to taking photographs of the award-winning ceremony at the annual dinner and had noticed that one of the trophies was in fact different at the 2017 dinner to the 2016 dinner. The problem was where had the original trophy gone? And why was there an apparently duplicate one? The situation had developed like this:

Michael, serial winner of croquet tournaments, was to be Master of Ceremonies for the croquet club dinner. This was to be held at the usual time in the year, but the format was to be different from previous years, in as much as that there was to be no 'top table'; guests would seat themselves randomly according to a 'draw'. Ordinary members would now be able to meet committee members, a process bound to strengthen 'club ties', wasn't it?

"This is pure social engineering!" Aunt Agatha

complained to Charles. "Can you imagine members jostling for places? Husbands and wives, lovers and sweethearts will be separated; there will be chaos!"

"Ah, but, you see, it was agreed at the committee meeting; and, also, that where a bottle of wine was shared between two people, they could sit together," Charles replied.

On the day of the croquet club dinner, members duly appeared, and were asked to pick a playing card from a pack which would be matched with a card of the same value on the table, and that would be their place. Four tables were laid with eight places on each. Members placed their bottles of wine in their selected spots, and that was when the precisely timed events started to unravel. Some members, who had wanted to sit with their spouses, found they could not sit with them as their places had been allotted to members with the appropriate 'playing card' number. Bottles of wine were un-united with their owners.

Charles said, "I knew this would happen!"

He was seated on one table and Aunt Agatha on another. One guest complained that she hated the person she was seated beside. Nevertheless, after a fractious fifteen minutes, everyone was seated more or less where they wanted and if they didn't, at least they were seated near to someone whom they regarded as being acceptable

The waiters came and asked, "Who was the soup and who was the pate and who was the prawn cocktail and who was the melon?" This took another half hour, and then the main course; this took further sorting, and another half hour. Some members started complaining their lamb or their chicken or their turkey was cold.

"I'm not coming again!" Aunt Agatha cried.

Meanwhile, in another part of the town, Mac, as he was known, an old surgeon and a member of Binchester CC, was a guest in a local care home and had heard there was a party on! He had persuaded the matron to issue him with an evening pass. He was a distinguished surgeon, coming from a long line of medical men. His profession was arduous, and like a lot of people working under pressure, he occasionally resorted to visiting the local hostelry with his chums. Of average height and build with a prominent brow, photographs of him at home saw him standing beside a fireplace with a bevy of young nurses arranged around him, a testimony to his popularity. On arriving at the dinner, he had seated himself, rather unwisely, in the chairman's place and proceeded to help himself to the chairman's bottle of wine! His wife, fearing the worst, began talking insanely to anyone who cared to lend her an ear.

Poor Anne Bee, the legal beagle had fainted amid scenes of some despair in the area around her. By the time the chairman (who was 'The Analyst') returned from the comfort station, and found his bottle of wine empty, and someone else in his place, all bedlam was let loose. Nevertheless, he managed to keep his sangfroid, and announced that, "The prizes will now be awarded."

Girl Katerday, seated beside Malcolm the Magnificent, looking resplendent in his new multi-coloured trousers and matching coat in the colours of the croquet balls, remarked, "What a good party this is!"

To which he replied, "Speak for yourself, madam!"

Johnny, Girl Katerday's other half, was not in evidence at this point but was later to be found snoozing in the corner by the bar, a half empty bottle of Schnapps in his hand.

"I don't think this was such a good idea," Peta remarked.

Rocky wisely agreed. Rich, local sage nevertheless also thought it was a good party and nodded knowingly to his wife, but got her name wrong which did not improve matters.

While this was going on, someone had panicked and had called for the ambulance. The call had gone through to the mayor's office – again! Deputy Mayor Bulldog Maclean, in situ. Bullock had only been in his post as Deputy Mayor for less than two months. He was standing in for his friend, General Battlin' Dave, who was on annual leave, and although now in a rest home was still able to carry out his mayoral duties. Together, they had served in conflicts all over the world. Bulldog was Dave's protégée. Bulldog's claim to fame was when he had organised the extraction of an important European CEO from jail and which had been made into a documentary. Bullock was a sunburned muscular no-nonsense go-getter, six feet three inches in height, eighty-five kilograms in weight, a Green Beret Colonel, equivalent to the SAS; clean-shaven with crew cut, he was the embodiment of the USA serving officer corps: 'Nothing is impossible!'

Bullock opened the conversation, "Yeah, whaddya sayin'? A body under the table? Is he dead? Yuh' cannot say?" To Frankie, he said, "What's wrong with these people? Can't tell if he's dead or not?"

"All right, buddy! Help is on its way!"

Soon to be heard was the screeching of a convoy arriving of two or perhaps three ambulances, escorted by half a platoon of soldiers armed to the teeth and who had positioned themselves in defensive positions around the club.

"You can't be too careful," the mayor had said.

The medics arrived into the dining hall, with stretchers, oxygen and defibrillators.

"Sorry, Gov," they said to The Analyst, who was reading the names of the prize winners. "There's an emergency on!"

They took away the legal beagle that had fainted, but omitted to find Mac, who, by now, was semi-conscious under the table, and had moved further under it, so as not to interrupt the proceedings, and to be more comfortable

After another half hour, the prizes had been awarded, and all then departed for home in various stage of repair. An hour later, Mac emerged from under the dining room table, unscathed and, apparently, none the worse for wear, and asked where he was. Everyone had gone home and the room was empty. But residing on his chest was a cup, in fact a trophy; it read:

Binchester Croquet Club One Ball. How did it get there?

Charles, on arriving home, remarked drily, "With entertainment like this, who needs to go to a show?"

Posted on the noticeboard of Binchester Croquet Club next day: December 6th, 2017.

MISSING: ONE TROPHY. The One Ball Trophy has gone missing. Would anyone finding this trophy please return it to the secretary?

On the following day, a further notice appeared on the noticeboard of Binchester CC. It read:

On further investigation of the mysterious missing One Ball trophy, it has been noticed that the trophy is, in fact, a crude replica of the original. Would the winner of last year's One Ball trophy please confirm to the treasurer that he handed in the correct trophy before this year's dinner?

Two days later, the following was posted on the noticeboard:

It has been confirmed that the trophy handed in by last

year's winner of the One Ball is, in fact, a forgery; this year's winner has also received a forgery. As the original trophy was made of solid silver, this represents a considerable loss, not least in monetary terms.

And, again, the following day:

A reward will be given to any person who can provide information that will lead to the recovery of the original cup. The matter has been reported to the insurers and the police.

The observant reader will have remembered that a *One Ball* trophy was found on the person of Mac unknown to himself; but is it the original? Of course, no one knows anything!

Arriving back at the care home at two a.m. the next morning, Mac, trophy in pocket, rang the night bell.

The night attendant exclaimed on seeing him, "Goodness gracious, Mac, where have you been? Do you know the time? We've notified the police and they have been out looking for you all over Binchester!"

"Well, as a matter of fact, I've been to a rather good party; I hadn't realised I've caused anyone any anxiety!" he said.

"Well, you had better get back to bed, and we'll see what happened in the morning."

Next day, Mac had difficulty remembering where he had been the previous evening. In front of him was the *One Ball* trophy, sitting on his bedside table.

"Well, my!" the day staff remarked. "Where did you get that trophy? It looks very handsome. We had better put it up on the shelf there."

During the next few days and weeks, Mac had a number of visitors. One of them happened to be Charles, who, noticing the trophy, said, "Mac, that is the missing trophy. How did you get hold of it?"

Mac said that he had not known how it got there, but that Charles could take it back and return it to the right owner. Charles did, but only to discover that the trophy he had returned was not the original one, but a fake replica made of tin. So where was the original one and who had swapped them?

Meanwhile, observers of the financial market scene would have noticed that the price of silver on the metal market had increased considerably in recent days; was Silver Fox, the mega-dealer behind it? Was he trying to corner the market? Were householders cashing in on their heirlooms? Had the Binchester *One Ball* Trophy been sold on the open market? Tongues wagged: was there a 'mole' in the club? Or, worse still, a 'ratty'?

The price of silver soared inexorably; the news was that Silver Fox was trying to manipulate the market. Until one day, sovereign nations decided to flood the market with their own hoards. Silver Fox, unable to buy this enormous amount, saw the price of silver crash in no more than one day. Unable to sell his enormous quantity of silver, Silver Fox lost one to two billion dollars and his credibility!

Next day, on the Binchester notice board appeared:

We now have three fake One Ball trophies; a reward of fifty pounds will be given to the person who can lead us to the recovery of the original One Ball trophy.

SPRING 2018

Analyst was over from St Helena for the season. He played croquet to a high standard, representing his county, Hampshire, and was also captain of Binchester CC, regularly taking part in the club's activities.

Despite the excitement over the missing trophy of the previous few days, life went on in an unperturbed way. The following day was the day of the Crazy Croquet Tournament. By popular demand, the captain had resurrected the tournament after one year of enforced absence due to an invasion of badgers on the lawn which had been damaged by their efforts in looking for choice pickings of 'leather jackets'. The two organisers, Glam and Princess Razzle-Dazzle were in full flow aided by Charles, an old lag who knew a thing or two about croquet. They were trying out a new version with a chess timer clock. As Charles was explaining 'it was about speeding up play…' when, suddenly, there was an enormous bang and explosion from very nearby. The players were rooted to the spot where they stood, as, over their heads flew the top of the 'old' croquet hut, which was now used for storage. There then followed an almighty whoooooosh of air, and in slow motion, the sides and then the front, followed by the back of the hut slowly toppled over, leaving a cloud of dust and debris settling in the cold frosty air!

What had happened? The captain playing in what had been a natty shade of pastel blue was now covered in a layer of grey ash, and looked as pale as a sheet.

Peta said, "Oh no!"

Rocky said he had seen this happen in films. Within the remains of the hut, standing bolt upright, a blackened figure could be seen, a wisp of smoke coming from the top of his head: it was Battlin' Dave.

He said, "Oh no; it can't happen to me!" He had left a tin of ammonium bitartrate in the hut on a bag of fertiliser; he must have lit a cigarette and the whole thing had gone up!

Worse was to come. Someone in the clubhouse had seen

what had happened and had summoned the fire brigade. It had rung in the mayor's office, for the fourth time that year! Deputy Mayor Bulldog Maclean was not pleased. "Frankie, come here!" he bawled. "S'one trying to take mickey out of me; deal with this, will ya?"

The mayor's secretary rung the fire brigade.

"Oh no!" cried the captain. "Not over the lawn, please!"

The fire brigade had taken their vehicle over the lawn with their hoses trailing alongside leaving the most hideous of marks.

"This will be the end of us!" wailed Johnny.

"You speak for yourself!" cried Malcolm the Magnificent, who thought of himself as Napoleon, who had been banished to the island of St Helena in the South Atlantic and somehow, had managed to escape in the hold of a visiting cargo ship and had reappeared on the playing fields of Binchester croquet club as himself. It was of course only an illusion!

Meanwhile, the redoubtable, Miss Ballantine, a member of Binchester CC, sensing trouble, had assigned herself to the case of the missing *One Ball* trophy; her reputation caused others to tremble in the underworld of petty crime. Miss Ballantine, the famous detective would leave no stone unturned in the search for the culprit. She retained her licence following the case at Truffles.

She concentrated her search now on General Battlin' Dave, he, with the military connections, hero of innumerable campaigns around the world, and now in retirement in Rainbow Court, Binchester. He had been the last known recipient of the *One Ball* trophy and had admitted to the explosion in the croquet hut. Miss Ballantine obtained a search warrant to Battlin' Dave's apartment. Had he any secret hobbies of dubious legality? She wanted to know.

"What a stink!" she said, on entering Battlin' Dave's apartment. "Is it ammonia? What are you doing, Dave?"

"Well," he observed. "I have my own experimental laboratory here. I am trying to synthesise silver from other elements. It's a hobby, you know, but at the moment, it is not going according to plan!"

Miss Ballantine looked round. On a shelf were numerous trophies, sporting cups, in fact. She looked more closely. Engraved on the side were the words *One Ball trophy, Binchester Croquet Club*, "But they are all in tin!" she cried.

"How very true!" Dave said, sadly. "That is because my experiments are not working. They all come out as tin!"

"This will have to stop, Dave, it is causing everyone a lot of headaches, what with the missing real *One Ball* trophy, and everything."

A few weeks later, Charles went to see Mac with a bag. Entering Mac's room, Mac observed, "What are you carrying in that bag, Charles?"

"Well," said Charles. "These are for you; there are sixty, *One Ball* trophies, all engraved with your name, reflecting the number of years you were playing croquet and winning trophies. Now, instead of having just the one trophy you brought with you after the croquet club dinner, you can now say to your visitors, 'these are all the trophies I won during my career', and you will be the talk of the town!"

"Well, I'm blessed!" Mac said.

Three months later in June 2018, it was the day of the captain's tournament. The weather was balmy, the mood relaxed. The 'clunk' of mallet against ball echoed across the 'close'. The smell of new mown grass hung over the air. The captain arrived looking; it must be said, rather sheepish. "You know what," he said. "I just found the real *One Ball* trophy in my kitchen cupboard; it has been used as an eggcup. I keep turkeys," he tried to explain.

CHAPTER EIGHT
Riot at Binchester CC!
Summer 2018: The Hottest Summer on Record!

The year 2018 had been a fantastically busy year in the life of Binchester Croquet Club: first of all, they found themselves unable to field a team versus the local opposition, lost a valuable cup, and had been at the epicentre of another public disturbance involving the Mayor of Binchester. All this, while the epic struggle with President Tyrinov had been going on, which had involved Peter Mikhail Czarevitch, Colonel Rich and others.

Despite her humiliation at the hands of the extraordinary meeting of the Binchester Country club when her motion to disband the croquet section was defeated by three hundred and thirty-eight votes to one, Ms Knowall was not finished, anything but! Not for nothing had she toiled endlessly for hours in the reading room of the International Economics School (IES) or attended endless seminars at the Student Union. She had been made an officer of the debating society and had recently been elected president. She had taken part in debates on student reform, reform of the election for fellows of the self-styled Opened-up University. She was a champion for social reform and Binchester Country Club was ripe for improvement.

At the next meeting of Binchester Country Club, there was again discussion on the future of the club including croquet; the chairman, General Battlin' Dave who had been brought out of retirement to fill in for Mr Shortsighted, had asked the chairwoman of the policy group to present her views on the future of the club.

"Well, as you know, General, apart from the issue of the croquet club, we should consider firstly the representation of the club on the board. We should reframe the voting procedure so that it is representative of the club. There are five hundred juniors, five hundred in the youth section, five hundred in the adult section and fifty in the seniors. The board is composed entirely of elderly men. There is one young woman only. We must change the representation of the board to reflect the composition of the club. For example, if the board has ten members, then three should be juniors, three youth, three young adults, and one senior."

Messrs Grouch, Scriabin, Shaker, Contract and Johnny, all long-time serving elected members of the board were reduced to a shocked silence; looking at first ashen, and then puce with rage, they, in effect, imploded as if they had been hit with an incendiary bomb. Attendants rushed in with carafes of water, whisky and smelling salts. The general's nurse was produced and his sedan chair brought out of retirement.

"Take me home!" he cried. "Never before in my long career, have I been experienced anything like this."

Indeed, such revolutionary ideas had not been heard of since the French Revolution.

"Ah, well, this is your chance, because this is going to be how it is here. Just you wait and see!" Ms Knowall exclaimed.

Another Extraordinary Meeting of the Binchester Country Club was called: top of the agenda was again:

1. Future of the Croquet Section.

2. Introduction of Modernist facilities.

3. Composition of the Main Committee.

Mr Shortsighted, who now took the chair, asked who was to present the first motion. "Ah," he said. "I see it is to be Ms Knowall; please do not be too long."

Five minutes later, Ms Knowall had just got to the meat of the matter. "Croquet is an elitist pastime; it is not a sport at all. The members are all well off, and have been to universities; there are no members from poorer sections of society. Not only that, they are subsidised by the main club. Their first-year subscription is only thirty pounds. I propose a vote that the croquet section is disbanded and replaced by a bowls section. At least they are likely to be inclusive."

This, to boos from the croquet members present. It was in vain that Johnny defended the croquet section.

"We have been here since the club was begun in 1907. There are already ten bowls clubs within five miles of this club. Our membership has increased by two hundred per cent in ten years," he said.

A vote was however taken. The motion was carried by one hundred and twenty-six votes to eighty. A subsidiary motion allowing the croquet section three months to show why they should not be disbanded was carried. A wag suggested that the meeting had been highjacked by Ms Knowall's cronies. This was not met with any amusement.

Was the first motion an indicator of what was going to

happen with the second motion?

The second motion was more heated than the first, which was to say that the temperature rose to just below boiling point. Ms Knowall again presented the second motion. She said that statistics showed that the percentage of 'modernist' people in any society was between one per cent and five per cent and that therefore there should be personal facilities for 'modernist' persons; Mr Grouch said he did not know what 'modernist' was and could she explain? Ms Knowall replied that if he did not know what she was talking about, he should not be there and went on to say that 'modernist' stood for 'modern' attitudes, and that, really, he should go and get educated.

Mr Grouch grew red in the face and said he did not need lectures from her. Anyway, he said that the expense would be enormous and that, for example, the current facilities were linked to male and female changing rooms and could not be moved. However, he admitted that the facilities were inadequate and he would agree to 'modernist facilities' at the far end of the building where there was space.

The tone of the meeting was evidently going to continue to be even frostier, as Malcolm the Magnificent alluded to Charles and they could expect more fireworks.

Motion three, proposed by Ms Knowall and seconded by one of her chief lieutenants, was that the club committee as at present constituted was illegal and should be changed.

Ms Knowall stated that all constitutions were now advocated to be representative of the sections and age differences of a club and that it was illegal to continually elect the same people to the same office. "As you know, Chair, at the last meeting, I said that membership of any committee should be proportional to the relative numbers of members in each section of the club: thus, we should have three juniors, three youth, three young adults, and one senior (over fifty-five years of age) member.

At this moment, a pin if dropped, could have been heard for miles around; suddenly, a hand was raised for a point of order by an elderly member who said, "Is it not in the guidance notes that members may introduce only one motion at a time at any meeting and not more than one…"

Ms Knowall cried out, "The member is out of order, this is a 'modernist space concept' and members may not interrupt!"

This produced an outburst of jeers from many ordinary members, "Rubbish!" they cried.

"Resign!" said others.

Ms Knowall then called for the ushers to eject the member who interrupted to more jeers and calls for her resignation.

Mr Shortsighted, now showing he was not as shortsighted as might appear from his name, but sensing trouble ahead called for a vote on the motion. "Hands up all those supporting the motion."

By this time, there were a number of people shouting and calling names, arms were raised which could have signified support for the motion or could have been expressing their displeasure at Ms Knowall. Anyway, Mr Shortsighted said, "Seventeen votes 'for' and…" when, suddenly, out of the blue, an object shot across the room: a flour bomb exploded on Mr Shortsighted's forehead, knocking him backwards on his chair such that he was temporarily put out of action. A scuffle then broke out on the floor, someone threw a punch, there was much shouting, and one member emerged holding a handkerchief over his bleeding nose. Some delegates from the UoDB

(University of Doggers Bank) had been bussed in by Ms Knowall to support her cause, and they had met with resistance from the ordinary members. There was more shouting, a chair, then another, came hurtling over the heads of some people. Ms Knowall was struck by a rotten tomato and had to be escorted out, shrieking; her supporters took matters into their own hands. Members were knocked to the floor; two gatecrashers from the 'No Bounds' anarchy brigade started shouting slogans and overturning tables, adding confusion to the deteriorating situation.

Malcolm the Magnificent, and Charles, together with other croquet members barricaded themselves in using upturned tables as a fortress. Mr Grouch who had also been knocked down managed to reach out with his free hand to ring the panic button.

It rang in the mayor's office for the fifth time in two years!

The Mayor's Office

"Phone for you, colonel," Frankie came in. "It is the Binchester Country club; they are ringing with another emergency; this is the fifth time in two years. They report a riot in progress!"

Bullock sprung upright, "OK, give me the line." Addressing the caller, he asked, "What seems to be the trouble? You're what? You can't tell me why. What? You are under the table with an anarchist on top of you! Leave it to us, buddy. We'll sort out any anarchist, we'll be right up there!"

"Gee, Frankie, get my Head of Cons-op." Frankie dialled the number and passed Bullock the phone.

"Hey, Bobbie, we got a spot of trouble up at the tennis club; seems a lot of anarchists are creating mayhem! Can your men sort it out?"

"Sure can, Bullock; I will send my best snatch squad." Bobbie, on his last tour of duty before retirement, went off to organise the team. Bobbie was five feet seven inches tall, sturdy as an ox, with tattoos over both arms. He was a 'go-getter' too.

Ten minutes later, three Humvee vehicles loaded with four men in each, fully laden with riot gear shields, taser guns, tear gas and other technological wizardry roared up the drive way to the tennis club. The anarchists of course knew this was about to happen and had already made their escape through the catering quarters; the Humvee teams meanwhile had covered all the other exits but had not taken into account the kitchen quarters and so missed their main target. Remaining in the hall were the delegates from the University of Doggers Bank (UoDB) plus all the club members including the croquet delegation.

The SWOT team stormed the meeting hall with a stun grenades and tear gas; Bobby's sergeant spoke to the members inside with a loudhailer, "Give yourselves up; you cannot escape!"

Of course, they were now a frightened bunch of inhabitants hiding under tables, who hardly had 'escape' in their minds, and who were already bruised and battered from the preceding brawl.

Names were taken, ringleaders, that is to say Mr Shortsighted, Mr Grouch, Ms Knowall and her chief lieutenants were handcuffed and led away; when a final rollcall was taken of the members present it was found that Malcolm the Magnificent was also missing.

A call was made to the mayor's office; Frankie answered,

"Yes," she knew where Malcolm was. "He is a guest of Her Majesty in Binchester Prison!"

IN THE GAOL

Queen Annie was upset! Having organised *Mixins* for several years, she now found her principal player was missing – that was how she liked to look at her players – as an orchestra. How could play continue without him? She spoke to her right-hand woman, Counsellor Wanda, and wondered if she could visit the offices of Messrs McMoo & Co to see if they could locate Malcolm the Magnificent. The counsellor duly went to the office to discover that Malcolm had indeed been detained. Anne of Islederney, Chief Clerk now in the offices of Angus McGoo & Co would investigate the reason for Malcolm's detention.

Later that day, Anne of Islederney of Messrs Angus McNoo & Co rang Annie Gee. "I have disturbing news! Malcolm the Magnificent is in gaol for riotous behaviour, inciting others to riot and aggressively wielding a mallet or hammer shaped club. He may be bailed for ten thousand pounds. I suggest the counsellor goes to see him to see if he needs anything. We may be able to help on medical grounds."

The next day, Wanda, the counsellor, visited Malcolm the Magnificent who was feeling anything but magnificent. He was in prison clothing, a drab sort of grey T-shirt and baggy grey trousers, looking very down at heel and mouth. "Look what they've done to me," he cried. "I am no better than a beggar in here. They don't listen to what I say. They just say, 'Oh yes, pull the other one!' What am I to do?"

"Well," the counsellor said. "We are trying to see if we

can get you out on medical grounds. Meanwhile, I have brought you some jelly babies and some woolly socks for the cold nights."

Anne of Islederney of Messrs McMoo & Co contacted Malcolm's medical advisers for a report on his general physical condition; it was alarming reading but could not be divulged on confidentiality grounds. It summarised, '*he should be released on medical grounds*' and a copy was sent to the prison authorities, who replied back that they too had obtained a medical report, and that this said that the prisoner was perfectly fit and responsible for his actions.

Consternation now reigned in the ranks of Queen Annie Gee and her subjects. What were they to do? They could not afford the bail and there did not seem any hope of releasing Malcolm the Magnificent on health grounds. Anne of Islederney of the law firm with the difficult name was not hopeful. He may have to serve his sentence. I will find out what this is likely to be. Next day, Anne of Islederney said that there was to be a hearing on Malcolm's case the following morning.

The following morning duly arrived. Malcolm the Magnificent was to be taken to the court, where Her Justice Lady Hildegarde Montmorency was sitting; the hearing, however, had to be postponed as Malcolm the Magnificent did not have his tablets and he had to go back to get them; when he did get them, they were the wrong ones.

The prosecuting attorney was not amused. "M'lud, I beg your pardon, m'lady. Can we have this hearing today in the prisoner's absence? He is trying to put off the hearing, m'lud?" he said.

The judge cast a beady eye over the attorney, this was not the way she was accustomed to being addressed. Reminding herself to get a note of the attorney's name, she agreed it was intolerable for the court's time to be wasted. "The prisoner will serve five years in jail."

The UoDB mob were given a twelve-month suspended sentence for being 'party to a riot'.

OUTSIDE THE GAOL

Queen Annie Gee summoned her principal lieutenants, Kathleen, fair and comely, the counsellor, Wanda, vivacious and lively, and Moira, the bonnie Scots lassie from Glasgow; they met together in the croquet hut. "We have a crisis, girls," the queen said. "How can we get Malcolm out? We don't have the money and if we leave him there for five years, heaven knows what mood he will be in by then! I don't think I can cope with this," she added as an afterthought to herself. They put their thinking caps on.

Kathleen said, "Maybe, we can have a bonfire and smoke him out?"

The counsellor said, "No, we need something more positive; a protest by the staff, social workers, probationers, guards, etc., and then in the confusion we can get him out?"

Kathleen also suggested, "I remember a bank heist on Easter day when a tunnel was bored under the vault when no one was there and all the cash stolen."

Someone else shouted "What about starving them of tea; after six months, they will be frantic!"

"How about a bomb under their kilts? That should create a stir," this from Moira.

"No, this will never do," said the queen. "Let's all think about it overnight, and come back again in the morning," she said, adding as an afterthought, "I wish I wasn't doing this!"

The next morning, the counsellor said, "I've been talking to Bobbie, and he said he had seen the documentary, in which Bullock Maclean had rescued a prominent business man from prison and, he said, why don't you go and speak to him to see if he will get Malcolm out?"

Now, even though Bullock Maclean was the temporary Mayor of Binchester, he was sworn to uphold the law. The queen said that Bullock would never help them, but the counsellor was insistent, "If you don't try, you will never find out!"

The queen conceded the point; she would take two of her supporters, Kathleen and the counsellor, to parlay with the Bullock. An appointment was made for five minutes to five by Frankie the following day. "You will only have five minutes," Frankie said. "He asked why you were coming, and I said it was about Malcolm. He asked who Malcolm was; I said Malcolm the Magnificent!"

The following day, the queen's delegation arrived at Bullock's office.

"Come," a stentorian voice from within the mayor's sanctum ordered.

The queen's troupe filed sheepishly in. "What can I do for you, ladies?" the stand-in mayor asked.

"Well, it's like this, our friend, Malcolm, is imprisoned wrongly; he is not strong and we are concerned his reason may go if he does not get his tablets."

"You are wrong there, the 'smart ass' has medical attention twenty-four hours a day, plus a nurse and medical orderly always on standby; anything else?"

"Well, yes," said the counsellor. "I've read you freed an

important European business man from prison; could you not do the same for Malcolm?"

"Wrong again," the deputy mayor shifted in his seat. "We did not free him; the prison was set alight and all the prisoners walked free and he just walked into our hotel. All we did was to take him to the Bahrani border. Anyway, who is this Malcolm, and why is he so 'magnificent' as you call him?"

"Well, er – it's like this – er…" the queen began.

The counsellor helped out, "It's his brain, actually. He has a brain, a very big one; he has had a hospital named after him 'The Grave Hospital'"

"No, actually; the Grove Hospital," the queen helped out this time.

Bullock replied, "I'm sorry I can't help you, but I will speak to the general." The interview was finished.

Two days later, a crowd had gathered outside Binchester Prison some one hundred yards away from the main gate. It was six p.m. and quite dark. A young woman dressed in a maroon trouser suit, Frankie, the temporary mayor's secretary was holding a banner; it read: *Yew Tree Film Studio Filming tonight – A Mock Break-in.*

Your former worship, Anne of Islederney of that ilk, also in maroon, had a large wooden box with 'Danger Mouse' printed on the side. Bobbie, the mayor's right-hand man held an extendable ladder and other stuff. He was in maroon, too, a kind of film studio uniform.

At exactly 6.05 p.m., an outbreak of cheering and noise came from the other side of the prison gate and what sounded like firecrackers; anyone standing there would have seen a recording and sound box with Bobbie's sergeant holding it.

Back at the prison; time 6.10 p.m., the Worshipful Anne

of Islederney loosened off an object that flew high over the prison wall – it was a drone! Underneath it, could be seen two small packages, one marked *Semtex* and the other marked, *Diamond Tipped Cutting Equipment*. It also signalled the coast was clear. Bobbie raised the ladder against the prison wall; another man unseen before, also in maroon, scaled the ladder; he was soon followed by Bobbie.

Amongst the general hubbub, in the distance, a long way away, a siren could be heard; perhaps it was an ambulance or a fire engine.

At this point, the main prison gate opened and a small grey man emerged holding a brown paper bag and supported by two sticks; he looked round, bemused perhaps, as if searching for someone who wasn't there, and started walking unsteadily in the direction of the film crew.

He arrived at the small crowd and seeing the queen said, "What are you doing here?"

Looking shocked, the queen replied, "What are *you* doing here? You are supposed to be in prison!"

"Well, they let me out because I was a nuisance to them," the small grey man replied. "They kept on giving me the wrong tablets." It was Malcolm the Magnificent!

Almost simultaneously, two sounds were heard; a muffled bang from somewhere in the prison quarters and also the siren which sounded much nearer. "Crikey, they're coming this way," cried the queen becoming alarmed. She said to Malcolm, "There's been a real 'horlicks'! We were supposed to rescue *you*, under the guise of a film crew. Did you not get our message? We sent you a drone with Semtex and Diamond Cutting Equipment for you to use. It is still up there somewhere and now it has all gone horribly wrong."

Two police cars arrived to a screeching halt. The queen yelled, "Scatter!"

She, along with Frankie, who dropped her banner, the counsellor and Moira ran across to the darkened side of the road. Malcolm retired to mingle with the crowd. Unfortunately, Bobbie, who was still perched up on the top of the wall, and Anne of Islederney and Kathleen who as usual was trying to help, but got in the way, were arrested and taken to be questioned in the police station.

It looked bad for all three of them. "A case of going from the frying pan and into the fire!" the counsellor said.

While all this was going on, five elderly gentlemen who initially had been arrested but had been released on bail, sat in a huff, contemplating their position in the croquet hut. The croquet hut had been recently demolished in an explosion set off by Battlin' Dave, retired Chairman of Binchester Country Club, but had now been replaced by a Portacabin. They sat in a row looking po-faced, facing the outside world like so many stuffed mannequins, looking out on the rain teeming down the windows outside; it is a matter of opinion whether they were just older than they looked, or just old and elderly. That was unimportant. What was possible was that they had been there for some time, even centuries, their lives snuffed out by volcanic ash as in Pompeii. No one inspected the hut to see if there was life there. If there was, it was only a sign of life now and then; an eyelid might flicker or an occasional involuntary movement of a limb occurred, which confirmed life existed. These elderly artefacts were in fact, Messrs Shortsighted, Grouch, Scriabin, Shaker and Contract, the former arrested members of the committee of Binchester Country Club. They were contemplating their dire position, more than whether they might get fed that day.

At the same time, in the café-bar of Binchester Country Club, Queen Annie and her team were worried; in the space of an hour, although Malcolm the Magnificent had been released, they had lost three other members of their team. To lose one might be considered careless, two unlucky, but three in the same team seemed positively negligent. The queen asked for their opinion as to what they might do. One by one they spoke up. Moira suggested they put a bomb under the prison authority's kilts which might shake them up!

"No, no!" cried Queen Annie. "You are only telling me what you told me before; go home and think about it and let me know in the morning!" To herself, she said, "No more please, no more; let me go home!"

In the croquet hut, something stirred, Mr Shortsighted moved a muscle; he read out a by-law from the Binchester Country Club Constitution. "Fifteen or more members may apply to have an Extraordinary Meeting of the Club, the meeting to be held within fifteen days of registering a request with the secretary. Gentlemen, we must act before we are taken over. I have already heard that the new committee wish to have a seminar room, a meditation room, a counselling room, a fruit machine and many more additions. You will remember that the motion for a new constitution was passed 'in absentia' at the last meeting, did we not?"

None of the other members disagreed.

Seven days later, both the Binchester Country Club and the local assizes met simultaneously to discuss the situation of the club and the fate of the three prisoners.

Seventeen members turned up at the EGM at Binchester Country Club; Mr Shortsighted said that the decision to accept the count of members supporting the motion to change the constitution should be null and void as a full count could not have been made owing to a riot taking place; The members agreed; however, in a valiant note of conciliation, Mr Shortsighted proposed that there should be a young member under the age of twenty-one on the committee. A subsidiary motion restored the croquet club as a legitimate section of the Country Club. As Ms Knowall was absent, it was recorded that she had left and applied for a job at another organisation, no doubt 'ripe for change.'

At the local assizes, the fate of the three prisoners held in the Binchester Prison was at stake. Ben Lyons, corner shop boy, reporter for the Daily Mercury was there. He wrote:

Justice Her Ladyship, Hildegarde Montmorency, has made the following landmark ruling:

'There are two things bothering me about this failed prison rescue attempt. The first is this: is it not a little ironic that her retired Worship Anne of Islederney (or wherever you come from), having spent many years sending people 'down', now finds herself in the very same position herself? Ha ha! The second strange thing is that there is a fourth person involved whom we have not been able to apprehend. We have found a mayoral badge in Malcolm the Magnificent's cell. How did that get there, I wonder?' Pause, then, 'I sentence the defendants, Bobbie, Kathleen and Anne of Islederney, to six months in prison or a one thousand pounds fine.'

The retired legal 'pro' Anne of Islederney, had smuggled out a note; she and the judge, Lady Hildegarde Montmorency, had been at school together, Sheltenham Lady's College, and had always been rivals for the top positions there, especially Head Girl! The rivalry had not dimmed over the years. The note, considered as relevant evidence, was read out by the

Court Clerk:

M'lud... m'lady, er... your lady, lordship... m'notmyladyluv... whoever you are. I have heard your unpleasant remarks, and I am ignoring them; but I was always better than you!

The Lady Hildegarde Montmorency increased her sentence by a further six months!

ADDENDUM

The person leading the assault on the prison was, of course, none other than Bullock Maclean who relishing one more chance to lead a prison breakout set off his own controlled explosion, entered Malcolm's cell, changed into a prison guard's uniform, summoned the guard, told them where the assailant was, and escaped via a circuitous route back to the mayoral chair. His diary does not record what his appointments for that afternoon were!

CHAPTER NINE
Islay
September 2018

Charles and Aunt Agatha were sharing a bottle of Prosecco and eating crumpets by the roaring fire in their period cottage. "I don't think I can take another week like the last one," Charles said. "Too much excitement with Malcolm the Magnificent being in prison, and then Anne of Islederney, Bobbie and Kathleen all being imprisoned too, I gather Kathleen so liked 'the good life' in prison, she has elected to spend her whole sentence there"

"Well, dear, you have better take it quietly because I've just been shopping and guess who I met?"

"No idea," said Charles.

"Malcolm the Magnificent I asked him how he enjoyed his stay in prison. 'Not at all', he said, 'the company wasn't to his liking!'"

It was the day of the Crazy Croquet Tournament; Princess Razzle-Dazzle (Dazzler) and Glam organised it by popular demand. The usual suspects were there: Analyst, Michael, (formerly Peter Mikhail, the newly anointed and virtual Czar, and also, formerly Sergeant Michel of the French Foreign Legion) – Peta and Rocky. Johnny and Charles. Two of the usual suspects were also missing – Anne of Islederney and Bobbie – did anyone know where they were? Sheepishly, the counsellor, Wanda, said she thought they were still enjoying the comforts of Her Majesty's hospitality.

It was to be a shotgun start; everyone was to start at the same time. Dazzler rang her bell. Everyone hit their balls – BANG! The balls were imitation balls filled with gunpowder! After that little excitement, things settled down to play Pirates, Random Golf Croquet and Target Golf Croquet. At the prize giving afterwards, Dazzler wondered if members had read the piece in the Croquet News suggesting that players might prefer to play competitions in 'coloured clothing' rather than 'whites' and she suggested that members might be asked for their views. This was agreed, and a questionnaire was sent out to members. This asked two questions: Firstly, if given a choice, would members prefer to play tournaments in coloured clothing or 'whites'? And secondly, what influences your choice?

Replies came in thick and fast! Answers were either, 'Coloured clothing over my dead body!' and 'about time too'. The result was twenty-six voted for coloured clothing and twenty-five votes against. At home, Charles said he had voted *for* coloured clothing, and Aunt Agatha said she thought that younger people would be more likely to take up croquet if they could wear coloured clothing, which now came in very smart and matching colours.

At the next *Mixin*, there was some heated discussion on the subject; the club was split as usual Charles thought, but fortunately there was no fisticuffs.

That night, Glam sent round a memo saying that her

birdwatching group would be on holiday, and would anyone like to join her? She would be away for a week; the event would be held on the island of Islay, off the south west coast of Scotland, where her great grandfather had been a cooper and she might even see some of his barrels. She would be going with the U3A members and her 'girlie' group, with whom she normally spent an annual week's holiday in some remote location.

Islay has many sandy beaches and coves, particularly at the south-western tip, where rugged cliffs overlook the ocean. It was here that 266 American sailors were lost when their ship HMS Tuscania was torpedoed in 1918. A monument commemorates them on the clifftop of Oa. Much of the island is moorland, which hosts sheep and cattle. Fifty thousand wild geese migrate there every winter; along with golden eagles, gannets, hen harriers, curlew, etc.

That was the idea anyway. After a week's thought, half the U3A members thought it was too cold and suddenly remembered that they had double booked the week, two called in ill with a bad cold, and the last member said that she thought that if she ever got there, the wild natives would not let her get out again unscathed. That left Dazzler, Harriett and Charlie, the two other members of the 'girlie' group.

"I think perhaps we should ask around to see if we can find any more members," Glam suggested. "I will email info@rent-a-group to see if any old hands might be around."

One day later, there were two replies; the first was Michael from Hampshire, England. Michael was a striking man in appearance; tall, very fit and off-puttingly muscular. The second reply was from Sam who was in Ireland. Sam is also fit, but not quite as fit as Michael. One wonders whether he goes to the gym?

Later that day, there was a third reply, from Ivan in London, who had a few days holiday and wanted a change of scenery. After working hard at ballet and becoming proficient, he had filled out and was very fit.

Glam thought the names were familiar. "Well, anyway," she said. "It would make life interesting!"

Their hotel's name was Port Charlotte, named after the mother of the builder, the former Laird of Islay. It is on the west side of the island; they would be staying in the whitewashed house, formerly three cottages and now a hotel. The area was famed for the wildlife around, both birds and animals.

The members of the group arrived in ones and twos, those from England, including Ivan, complained that they had to wait four hours for their flight and then got held up in Glasgow, owing to an 'incident' there, which was a false alarm, but which had all the police, emergency crews and ambulance men standing round for hours doing nothing. Glam said she wanted a hot water bottle to take to bed, as after the long journey, she felt chilly. The Dazzler asked if she had she done her forty minutes exercises for the day. Glam thought she had, as the effort of arriving was sure to be worth any number of forty-minute exercises.

They went down to the cosy lounge; an open fire with logs in place was burning brightly, and to their surprise, two more guests who had been touring Scotland, and had been there for a day or two, were there. They were none other than Charles and Aunt Agatha.

"My dear," Aunt Agatha said. "This is a small world!"

Charles said, "Did you know I am a member of the

Laphraig Whisky Society, and I've come to look at my own private piece of soil? Did you know that Islay had nine distilleries? All my favourite distilleries are here! Did you know that whisky was the main product?"

Of course, they had no idea, or said they didn't; any way, they were here to look at the birds.

Michael from England and Sam who had flown in from Ireland had been booked in to Bowmore House, right by Bowmore Distillery; they thought they were booked in to the Port Charlotte Hotel and found themselves in the Bowmore! Had the bookings been mixed up? The next morning, Michael and Sam attended the 'team talk' that had been arranged for the birdwatchers. There was to be a visit to a distillery in the morning followed by touring the island and birdwatching in the afternoon. In the Port Charlotte Hotel, the same 'team talk' was held. Each morning was to be devoted to birdwatching followed by lunch at one of the island's hotels and sightseeing plus a visit to a distillery in the afternoon. Was this another mix-up?

Michael and Sam decided to visit Bowmore Distillery which was on their doorstep, the oldest distillery on the island, and was established in 1779. Sam sampled the Bowmore number one, redolent of cinnamon, vanilla and matured oak and pronounced it 'very good!' Since the weather was bracing, but not unduly cold due to the influence of the Gulf Stream bringing its warm waters to the west coast of Scotland, they decided to spend the afternoon at Bowmore again, where Sam sampled the twelve-year-old Bowmore and pronounced it even better! Supplied with Drambuie and similar drams, they made their way back to Port Charlotte Hotel where to their surprise, they met up with the birdwatchers; Glam was especially surprised to meet Sam, who was her husband and whom she thought was in Ireland on business. He said that he had a change of heart and decided instead to join his wife on the island. The birdwatchers had been birdwatching that day, and had traipsed through wild mountain moorland, mud-flats, and mixed woodland, got thoroughly wet, and covered with mud; they were so exhausted, they had forgotten to look for what they had come for. In the afternoon, they had returned to their hotel to get dry and recover their poise.

Their poise recovered after a splendid supper of Rannoch soaked venison, Islay beef and ale stew and sticky toffee pudding. Afterwards, it was noted that Charles had established himself at the bar and was inviting anyone who cared to, to have a dram with him.

After everyone had retired, well-seasoned you might say, Glam had a dream; she found herself suspended by a halter and rope from a helicopter, which was hovering some one hundred feet above a rocky outcrop on the mountainside, and she was just inches away from a golden eagle's nest, the owner of which was regarding her malevolently with two beady eyes. 'Was she the eagle's next lunch?' the eagle seemed to be asking. 'Yes!' She awoke with a start; it was only a dream, wasn't it? She tried to go back to sleep, but found it difficult.

The next morning, post full Scottish breakfast, Michael and Sam said that their programme said they were to tour Bunnahabhain Distillery that morning. "That can't be so," said Dazzler. "We are to go there this afternoon!"

The confusion over whether to visit a distillery in the morning or afternoon was defused when Michael announced that he had never really liked whisky and he proposed to take the low road and walk while the others could go by the hotel minibus; in that way, he would see the wildlife. The 'girlie' party, including Glam, agreed to walk with Ivan and Michael; Dazzler would go by minibus, with Sam and Charles. Agatha decided to stay at home to sample the tea and cakes, which would take her most of the day! Charles noted that it took two and a half hours by road to get to Bunnahabhain, by walking. However, the road was new, so they might get there by sunset.

Bunnahabhain was on the north-east coast, on Margadale River, from whence it derived its pure unpeated water and the scenery was spectacular along by the seashore. They saw dolphins and seals, and maybe a whale or two. Bunnahabhain had originally been supplied by sea in little 'puffer' boats from Glasgow which both supplied the distillery with coal, and took their precious whisky to the mainland. Now the new road made the boats unnecessary and there were plans for a modern day upgrading of the distillery. Sam thought this was all very enjoyable. By the time they reached the distillery, it was nearly lunchtime, so they piled into the visitor centre. Sandwiches were to be had; Sam sampled a 'Toiteach A'Dha' whisky and Charles a 'stuireadair'. Both pronounced them very acceptable.

Later, a telephone call was made to Bunnahabhain Distillery saying that the remaining members of the party were stranded on the hills some five miles from Bunnahabhain, and were not amused as they were tired and hungry and could someone come and rescue them? By this time, it was six o'clock in the evening, and the party at Bunnahabhain were well lubricated as they stumbled into the minibus, singing well-known old songs. Glam was not pleased when they finally arrived at the point where her party had collected on the road.

"Sam," she said. "Don't you ever dare to leave me behind again!"

Arriving back at the hotel, everyone bathed in the peat coloured water, which was surprisingly refreshing and tempers were cooled when they sat down to supper, to a meal of pan-fried Scottish salmon fillet, lemon and parsley sauce, with Sauternes wine followed by a Bailey's Panna Cotta and Monbazillac liqueur.

Everyone slept well apart from Dazzler who had a dream that she was being targeted by a band of hooligans in the Kalahari Desert in South Africa and she had a bad fright as she had a real experience of the same in the Californian desert some thirty years ago.

The next day, day three of their tour, members elected to go to Lagavulin on the south coast in the morning and Laphroaig in the afternoon; Michael said he would go for a training run. Sam said he had no need of training as he was fit enough anyway, while Charles thought that any amount of additional exercise would do him great harm. Aunt Agatha said she would go with the crowd and the other members of the birdwatchers said they would go 'whisky hunting' today if they could have the whole day tomorrow to birdwatch. That agreed, the troupe set of for Lagavulin.

Lagavulin was a pretty distillery situated between Ardbeg and Laphroaig; it took thirty minutes to get there in the minibus. After dismounting, they all headed for the shop where they had refreshments, which in Sam's and Charles's case amounted to a sampling of their standard sixteen-year-old malt, which they both pronounced as being scrumptious! Lagavulin was now owned by Diageo which owned the largest number of breweries in Scotland. Previously, Lagavulin had a reputation for producing illicit whisky as far back as 1742 or maybe earlier. Their whisky was very peaty with a taste of iodine which was not to everyone's taste if they had just begun drinking whisky. It could safely be used as an excuse for being 'medicinal'!

After a lunch of sandwiches and a tipple or 'topple' or two, because, by now, they were fairly well lubricated, they sallied off to Laphroaig. Charles said he owned a bit of Laphroaig, One square foot in total and that he was a friend too and he had come to claim his inheritance.

"That sounds a tall story," they all said.

Glam said that her great, great and great grandfathers, James and David Burton Galloway – JBG or DBG – were coopers and she expected to find their names etched on some barrels there: It so happens that the original owners were Johnston's, Donald and Alexander Johnston so it would be very likely that Sam, whose surname was Johnston might find some connection here as well. Laphroaig has its own peatbog of heather, lichen and sphagnum moss which contributes to its unique medicinal taste.

Glam sought out the museum curator and told him her story.

"Certainly," he said. "There might be some old barrels in the museum. Go and look!"

Which they did, and low and behold, there in the corner were two barrels with the initials JBG and DBG faintly etched on the side. "My day is made," she said. "James and David Burton Galloway, JBG or DBG!"

That night, Michael had a disturbing dream. He believed he was told that he was the heir to the Russian throne, none other than the Czarevitch. And also, that he had been in the French foreign legion under the name of Sergeant Michel. How could it be? Yet it seemed so real. Glam and Princess Dazzler suppressed a knowing smile.

The next morning was free. Michael had gone to Glasgow by the ferry to play croquet at Kelvin Park for the day. Dazzler said that they, Glam, Harriet and Charlie, were going to go to Kildalton chapel, where there was a Celtic High Cross and they would do some bird spotting too. That left Charles, Sam and Ivan. They would go to Ardbeg Distillery where they had booked a two-hour tour. Aunt Agatha said she would stay in the hotel in the warm and have some more of their tea and cakes.

The tour was a great success. Ivan, Sam and Charles seemed to have a natural instinct for anything about whisky. When they arrived at Ardbeg, they were given a short history of the place. Ardbeg was owned by Glenmorangie which was itself owned by Louis Vuitton Moet Henessey. They then toured the buildings to see the process of making whisky. The first process 'malting' where the grain is dried with peat smoke to produce a 'grist' is now done at Port Ellen, a little further down the coast. Hot water is then added and the whole transferred to a copper heating tank (the 'mash tun') to produce a warm sugary liquid. The resulting 'wort' is cooled and yeast added, and then distilled twice, run through a condenser and put into oak casks for the final maturation to produce 'whisky'. This, then, was laid down for up to fifty years.

They then refreshed themselves with lunch in the café, assisted by a few drams of Ardbeg ten-year-old malt and Ardbeg Perpetuum and Exploration. At about the same time, Dazzler and friends had set off for Kildalton Chapel without looking at the weather forecast, which was a mistake as a weather front was moving in from the Irish Sea. Soon, the visibility had shrunk to a mere fifty yards. Any hope of arriving at their destination were soon dashed. No birds were seen that day, even the Celtic Cross was never glimpsed. Somewhat chastened, they decided that if they couldn't win, they would at least join the others at Ardbeg, which they did and had a very enjoyable lunch there.

The next day was their last day on Islay; they had visited all the distilleries they had time for, bar one, and seen no birds except possibly one. This was not how it was meant to be. It was decided, or rather, Princess Dazzler decided, that in the morning they would go Bruichladdich Distillery, have lunch there, and then all go on to Loch Guinant where the Barnacle Geese came every year from Greenland; in the evening there was to be a ceilidh!

Along the coast from Port Charlotte is Bruichladdich Distillery. It used to be privately owned until Remy Cointreau bought the company in 2012; however, it is still extremely independently minded! It gets its water from the farm of James Brown at Octomore and its barley from nineteen barley farmers over seventeen farms on the island. The Wood Brothers dry their barley at Octofad farm. Bruichladdich distil three different spirits, Bruichladdich (unpeated – unusual for Islay), Port Charlotte (heavily peated) and Octomore (the most heavily peated in the world!) Nonetheless, the 'experts' liked the whisky's lightness. The distillery used to have coal supplied by the Glasgow 'puffers.'

After a packed lunch supplied by Port Charlotte's kitchens, it was off to Guinant Loch; a track takes the visitor through some sheltered woodland to the viewing platform and Kilnave Chapel where a bloody war was waged between Sir Lachlan Maclean, 14th Chief of Duart and Sir James Macdonald of Islay in 1598.

Two thirds of the areas are mud flats and salt marsh; here in the winter, some eighteen thousand barnacle and white fronted geese come from Greenland for the winter. At the same time, Brent geese and whooper swans fly in from Iceland; also, to be seen are teal, wigeon, shovelor, marsh harrier, sandpiper and even peregrine and hen harriers.

Glam was especially delighted to see a mid-air food-pass by the hen harriers; there are stags and otters and the endangered marsh fritillary butterflies too.

"That was fun!" they exclaimed when they got home.

That evening, the ceilidh took place; all residents were invited to dress up in the guise of a bird. Michael was an albatross, Charles a heron and Aunt Agatha a duck which was her nickname. Glam was a hen harrier and Dazzler was a peacock while Ivan dressed up as a peregrine. Harriet and Charlie, of whom we have heard little, were nevertheless rather taken with Ivan, who was 'single,' they said, and that they could be interested if the opportunity... They were also determined to make their mark and came as 'golden-eye and 'pintail shovelor' birds which were very becoming. The music was supplied by J. MacCure and his band and was very merry; food from the Port Charlotte larder was plentiful as was the liquid refreshment. After many Scottish dances, the Gay Gordons and the Eightsome reel being prominent, a young female singer finished off the evening with a rendering of some favourite Scottish ballads, after which the members yawned and staggered off to bed.

Next morning, Glam said to Charles that they had missed out on three of the distilleries, Caol Ila, Kilshoman and Ardnahoe. And what should they do about it?"

Charles said, "Why, we must visit them next year!"

CHAPTER TEN
Full Circle

A LEVEL PLAYING FIELD

A level playing field is the industry standard model for decision making by negotiators and policy makers everywhere. Where all the available information is in front of the delegate, one might expect a result to satisfy most people, assuming both parties are acting in good faith; regrettably, sometimes this is not always the case.

In the arena of sports fixtures, a physically level playing field is assumed in field sports such as lacrosse, football, hockey and rugby to take some examples. If the sports ground is not entirely level, no one pays much notice as the result will not generally be affected, unless, say, a bowler bowling from the Gasholder End at the Oval can extract extra bounce or swing in his action, in which case, the opposition may grouse a bit.

In the case of some other sports like bowls and croquet, a level playing field is essential, and if it is not, then the players are very likely to complain. In the case of Binchester Croquet

Club, there is a definite inequality in the level of part of the playing surface. There is an area, in the shape of a gentle slope, between two hoops, some twelve feet across and some twenty yards in length which is two inches above the rest of the playing surface. This is the Winchester Hill. This 'hill' has been the scene of some controversies in the area, the local players having a distinct advantage over any visitors. For example, the local player may concede the preceeding hoop in order to win the next one. He will leave his ball beside the first hoop, in order to ascend the hill to the second hoop from the side, thus obtaining a good position to win the next hoop, whereas the visiting player thinks he has hit a perfectly good shot to find his ball trickling off the side of the hill to a useless position.

TIME: THE PRESENT

It was mid-summer; the cows sang, the birds mooed – it was mid-summer madness! The Binchester members, having now either returned from their summer holidays or about to go, resumed their hobby or sport on their finely tuned lawns. Thwack, thwack resounded ball off mallet, cheer and 'oooh' and 'that was a nice piece of sponge cake'. It was harvest time for off-the-shelf mid-lifers determined to garner in the best fruits of their remaining years.

The temperature rose, the air became humid; some of the least fit members perspired profusely or went home; it was the season for thunderstorms and lightning strikes, when one did just that. An approaching wind announced the arrival of at least a rainstorm; but in fact, it was a metallic object that descended like an out of space experience to the centre of the lawn – a drone, no less!

Many had not seen one and were frightened; pulses raced and some fell to the ground in half belief of a divine intervention.

Hilary Ballantine of private investigator fame said 'not to worry'. It was her shopping list which had just arrived! She now did her shopping this way and 'wasn't it convenient?' As if that wasn't expected, a second heralding of a further impending storm was heard over the tennis courts and a second drone dropped silently on to the lawn. There was a bit of a hush. Hilary walked over to it. There was a note attached. She began to read, "From Ivan. I have just got..." Before she could finish, the much-anticipated rain arrived and washed the writing off the note. It could not be read.

Ivan was the false Czar on the island of St Helena; after he accepted an invitation from Peta to join the Binchester Croquet Club, he stayed with Peta and Rocky for a year. After that, he accepted an invitation to lodge in Charles's son's flat in Pimlico, London, in return for carrying out household duties. During the week, he took dance classes at the City Dance Studio, and at the weekend he came down to Binchester to play croquet, and had reached a good standard by the end of his third year.

At the City Dance Club, you can learn all kinds of dancing from salsa to ballet, from ballroom dancing to jive; Ivan was particularly keen on ballet as he had a natural grace and fluency, as well as being very athletic and supple. He had, after all, learned ballet as a youngster in Moscow before being picked to be a decoy for the attempt to restore the Czar. He soon picked up on the basic ballet positions such as *a la barre,* the *pas de chat*, and moved on to the more complicated *glissade and arabesque*. He got the attention of his teacher who encouraged him to enter for the first-year prize which would enable him to win a scholarship that would pay for his fees. He duly won this and was soon getting the attention of the principal of the college. He learned the *cabriole* and *grande battement* and was soon doing *grand jetés*, very advanced jumps which received the admiring glances of many of the female artistes. By now, after some nine years or so of hard work, Ivan was twenty-five years of age; he was strong and athletic with good looks to match.

Ivan had also joined the British-Russian cultural club where he met some of the dancers from the Russian Ballet School in London, and he went to the Russian school once weekly, where he picked up some of the Russian emotional intensity at which they excelled. He also came to the cultural club once weekly to have lunch and which gave him the opportunity to socialise. On one occasion at the cultural club, he noticed four people coming in for lunch. There was a pretty young woman with a young man who seemed to be her companion, and two other gentlemen, who seemed to be in an official capacity. They looked as if they might be security guards; they were burly looking, and in dark suits and sunglasses, not that there was any sun. He later learned they wore sunglasses to avoid identification. At any rate, his attention was taken up by the young woman, and he wondered who she was.

Ivan continued to apply himself to improving his technique; on the occasion of his twenty-sixth birthday, he was surprised to receive a note from the principal asking to see him in his office. Not, without some nervousness, Ivan presented himself at the principal's office and waited. Was he going to be made redundant? Had he offended someone? He did not know; he could not think of anything wrong he had done!

The principal arrived. "Ivan," he said. "I have good news for you; I want you to be a principal dancer."

Ivan could not believe what he was hearing. To be a principal dancer was the highest of good fortune, the top of the tree.

He staggered out of the office, went home to Pimlico, and told Charles' youngest son, of his good news.

"Well," the youngest son said. "We must celebrate; by chance, I have a bottle of champagne in!"

After that, Ivan went around in a trance. He stood in for the first principal dancer when he was not dancing. Ivan continued to impress with his performance and, after a further two years, was offered the role of Count Albert in Giselle as first principal dancer. He was naturally nervous, but he knew he could do it.

The night of the first night arrived; his dancing coach held his hand. "You will be fine!" she said, and he was.

The audience gave five encores and clapped madly at his *jetés en menage.*

Ivan then took a few days holiday to go to the Island of Islay with a few of his friends from the croquet club. He was now twenty-eight years old, and the year was 2018, eleven years after arriving on the island of St Helena.

On his return, he was at the British Russian Club when the young lady, who he had remembered seeing before on a visit to the club, came up to him and said she had been to the performance of Giselle and loved his 'leaping', and was as quickly gone again leaving a trail of turning heads especially one from Ivan who rather hoped he might see her again!

An opportunity arose a few days later when they almost crashed into each other in the entrance foyer to the British-Russian Club. "Oh, I'm so sorry," he stammered. Looking into her eyes, he noticed how blue they were and added, "I was wondering... perhaps we might..."

When her phone went. Trrrring Trrrring... Trrrring Trrring.

"Yes, it's me, what is it? What! You wish me to come directly to HQ?"

She shoved a hastily written note into Ivan's hands. And she was gone, all shimmering in a blaze of gold and silver, as the sun settled down in the early evening light shining through the London plane trees.

She disappeared into a chauffeur driven Mercedes with the same two men he had seen her with before, who must be security guards.

Ivan's heart raced. *She must be important*, he thought. *Probably too important for her to see me again.* He still didn't know her name! She seemed too distant, too remote, too unreachable. Then he remembered the note she had thrust into his hand. He read it, it said: 07966121212.

"Come in, Tatiana," requested the chief of staff to BI10. "Your cousin, Mishka, will be here immediately. The chief has ordered you both to be moved at once for your safety. Electronic surveillance has noticed an increase in traffic in this area. Mishka arrived and was told the news. You will be going up north. I can't tell you where, but you will know soon enough. A conveyance will collect you at six p.m. this evening."

This was a bombshell to Tatiana in particular. "But I've just met... er... someone, and I rather hoped to..." she protested.

"All right we'll give you until the same time tomorrow evening, but there can be no further extension. There is a bit of a flap on!"

Ivan himself was also in a bit of a flap! She had left him a phone number! Was it a false number to throw him off the trail? He had no reason to think she was interested; on the other hand, she had given no indication to him not to follow her – no, he would not do that – or to desist from contacting her. On the other hand, she had given him her telephone number, so there must be a reason for that. She could be playing a game 'hard to get' he mused. Well, he could not spend all day wondering about the consequences; he would give her a ring, but when?

He would leave it overnight in the hope that sanity might prevail. Of course, that meant a sleepless night and he had his contract to keep to; he did not have much time and so decided to ring the next morning. At least he would know one way or the other.

Brring Brring… Brring Brring… Brring Brring… Brrring Brring…

A pause… then a quiet voice, "Hello?"

From Ivan, "Hello; it's me, Ivan. Is that – oh gosh – I don't even know your name. I'm so sorry; you must think me terribly rude?"

"Ivan; don't be silly. I've been wanting to meet you, quite apart from your dancing."

Ivan felt so relieved. "Perhaps we might meet somewhere?" he said.

"Yes, of course, but not here, I am in what is called a 'safe house'. And my name is Tatiana. Do you live near here?"

Ivan thought. The only place he knew was his room in

Winchester St. Pimlico, and she might not appreciate that, so he said, "Let us meet in Grumbles Restaurant in half an hour?"

Tatiana thought that would be fine; she knew it and had been there before. Facing each other over the table, Ivan studied her. He noticed the upturned corners of her mouth as if a perpetual smile, the gentle curve of her chin, her eyes, still blue and penetrating, her brow however had worry lines, but most of all, on her neck there was a substantial scar, healing now, but where there had been a gash caused by some injury he could not begin to know what it was. Tatiana caught him looking at it.

"Have you not been reading the papers, Ivan? It has been all over them. I and my cousin were the victim of a nerve agent attack three months ago, Phenichem. We were unconscious for one month in Exeter Hospital. We were poisoned in New Street, Honiton. That is why we are in safe houses. I am still not fully recovered."

Ivan was shocked; he had read about it, of course, but had not realised it was so close to home and he was talking to the victim. It took him some time to recover and ask why she had been attacked.

"I was a stenographer to the Central Communist Committee in Moscow. We would take notes of the proceedings, which were a rubber stamp of what was decided in the Politburo. It was public knowledge. All I did was to pass on copies of the meetings to the British Attaché in Moscow before he got them in the papers. It was quite innocent, but the authorities didn't like it, and they don't forget. They will get you in the end and that is what happened. I am lucky to be alive. But let's not talk about that. I am to be moved up north this evening and I wanted to spend some time with you."

They had the rest of the lunch in silence, Ivan absorbing

the immensity of what he had heard. There did not seem to be anything he could say which would help the situation. The scar on her neck was where she had a throat operation to help her breathing while she was unconscious; her cousin had been worse off and had been unconscious for longer, but fortunately, he was on the mend too, and he would be moved up north with her.

After a while, he thought that perhaps she might like to see where he lived and sit quietly until the time arrived for her to catch her transport north. She agreed and was content enough to walk the short distance to Ivan's rooms in Winchester Street, Pimlico. He made her some English tea and they chatted about his next role and his plans. Did he want to return to Russia? Did he have friends or relatives there? He did not know as he thought of himself as an orphan.

Suddenly, she leant forward and kissed Ivan on the cheek; though somewhat shocked, Ivan did not draw back, but put his arm round Tatiana's shoulders. She snuggled a bit closer and Ivan kissed her on the lips. She put one leg round his. The fragrance of jasmine permeated through the open window and the warmth of the sun added its comforting embrace to Tatiana and Ivan. He murmured, "I think in time I might be able to love you."

She whispered, "Me too."

It was time to go; the official BI10, but unmarked car, a Mercedes, arrived to take Tatiana back to her safe house to pack her few belongings. She thought they may be able to communicate by a box number, but it would have to be approved by BI10.

As time went on, they were able to communicate via PO boxes; certainly not electronically which would have been picked by the FSB or anyone else eavesdropping. Her health improved, as did the health of her cousin; Ivan became a national figure; he duly proposed and was accepted by Tatiana. A small private wedding service was held in the Russian Orthodox Church in Wick, Caithness with her cousin to lead her down the aisle. Those illuminati of the Binchester Croquet Club who could attend did so.

Afterwards, Tatiana said, "Where shall we spend our honeymoon?"

Ivan showed her some photographs of St Helena and said, "Well, what about St Helena; that is where it all began for me, and now, it could be for you too!"

"Good idea," Tatiana said.

THE ANNUAL CONVENTION OF THE GHOSTS; THE YEAR IS 2050

All enter from different parts of the forest.

Ghost of Charles said, "When I first became a ghost, I did a world tour; I also went back to Binchester Croquet Club; as I passed the tennis courts, I came across a wall near where the croquet lawns were. I went through the wall, and the croquet lawns were on the other side."

Ghost of Aunt Agatha asked, "Did you think they had gone?"

Ghost of Peta said, "I think they must have sold them."

Ghost of Rocky confirmed, "Yes, because there was always a right of way from the house opposite."

Ghost of Battlin' Dave said, "I do odd jobs now."

Ghost of Anne Bee chipped in, "I organise the other ghosts."

Ghost of Annie Gee said, "And I collect the money."

Ghost of Malcolm the Magnificent continued, "I find life difficult."

Ghost of Dazzler questioned, "Did you know about the

wedding?"

Secretary Ghost of Glam said, "OooOooOooOooh tell me, Dazzler!"

Ghost of Michael asked, "Could you fill in? Someone let me down."

Ghosts of Perpetuum and Analyst were seen discussing the latest croquet laws in a glade in the woods.

After that, they all disappeared to the far corners to await the next meeting.

Secretary Ghost to arrange the next meeting.